Also by Michael Delaney
Deep Doo-Doo
Henry's Special Delivery
Not Your Average Joe

DEEP DOO-DOO AND THE Mysterious E-mail

DEEP DOO-DOO
AND THE
Mysterious E-mail

by
Michael Delaney

Dutton Children's Books ■ *New York*

ACKNOWLEDGMENTS

I would like to thank Archie Adams, Nicholas Cooper, and Alex, Jamie, and Mackie Glashow for reading the story when it was in manuscript form. I am also very grateful to Melissa St. John for her advice on the Internet-related parts and to Susan Rand for suggesting that I throw a girl into the picture this time around. Somewhat belatedly, I'd like to thank Richard DiLallo for his helpful suggestions on the first *Deep Doo-Doo* book.

Library of Congress Cataloging-in-Publication Data
Delaney, M. C. (Michael Clark)
    Deep doo-doo and the mysterious e-mail / by Michael Delaney.—1st ed.
        p. cm.
    Summary: Instead of scooping a classmate who works on the school newspaper, Bennet and his friend Pete end up working with Elizabeth to find out who is responsible for putting a pumpkin on top of the town hall flagpole.
    ISBN 0-525-46530-8
    [1. Journalism—Fiction. 2. Friendship—Fiction. 3. Mystery and detective stories.] I. Title.

PZ7.D37319 Df 2001
[Fic]—dc21   00-056969

Published in the United States by Dutton Children's Books, a division of Penguin Putnam Books for Young Readers 345 Hudson Street, New York, New York 10014 www.penguinputnam.com

Designed by Richard Amari
First Edition
Printed in USA
10 9 8 7 6 5 4 3 2 1

To Lucia Monfried
and
Wendy Schmalz

CONTENTS

DEEP DOO-DOO AND THE Mysterious E-mail

LATE-BREAKING STORY

When the phone rang, Bennet was at the kitchen table, eating breakfast—a bowl of Frosted Flakes. He was scribbling on a yellow notepad as he ate. He was making a list of the things he thought were the most important issues facing North Agaming, the town he lived in.

"Bennet, could you get that?" his mother yelled from upstairs.

Bennet shoved a spoonful of cereal into his mouth, rose, and went over and picked up the phone by the refrigerator.

"Hulpho," he said, his mouth full of Frosted Flakes.

"Is this the Ordway residence?"

It was Trombly—the editor-in-chief of *The Sun*—the newspaper that Bennet's father worked for.

Bennet swallowed. "Hi, Mr. Trombly," he said. "This is Bennet."

3

"Oh, hey, Ben," said Trombly. "I didn't recognize your voice. How's the brain behind the Deep Doo-Doo broadcasts doing today?"

"Okay," said Bennet.

"Haven't been interrupting any TV signals, have you?"

"No."

"Glad to hear it," said Trombly, with a laugh. "Is your dad there?"

"J-j-just a minute," said Bennet, setting the phone down on the counter.

Bennet hurried out of the kitchen and bounded up the stairs. He entered his parents' bedroom. His mother was making the bed. She had already taken her shower. Her hair was wrapped in a towel, and she had on a dress and Nike running shoes. Bennet's mother always wore running shoes to work. She taught English at the junior high school.

"Who is it?" she asked, glancing over at Bennet.

"Trombly," replied Bennet.

"You mean *Mister* Trombly."

The door to the bathroom was closed. The shower was running. Bennet banged on the door.

"Hey, Dad, phone!" he shouted.

"I'll call back!" his father's voice yelled over the gushing water.

"It's Mr. Trombly!" shouted Bennet.

The shower snapped off. "Oh, for Pete's sake!" Bennet heard his father grumble in the bathroom.

The bathroom door opened, and Mr. Ordway stepped out. He was a short, middle-aged man with a bit of a paunch. Wrapped in a towel, he walked past Bennet, leaving a trail of damp footprints across the soft, beige carpet. He picked up the phone on the small table beside the bed.

"Hi, Bill," he said pleasantly enough.

Mr. Ordway listened for a moment. Then he burst out laughing. "You're kidding me!" he cried. "A pumpkin?" He listened again. And then he said, "I'm on my way," and hung up.

"What's up?" asked Mrs. Ordway.

"Late-breaking story," said Mr. Ordway. "Someone stuck a pumpkin on top of the Town Hall flagpole."

"A *pumpkin?*" said Mrs. Ordway, in disbelief. "How on earth did someone do that?"

"Don't know," replied Mr. Ordway.

"Who would have done such a thing?"

"Don't know that, either," said Mr. Ordway. "But I intend to find out. Trombly wants me to cover the story." He went back into the bathroom, closing the door behind him.

"C-can I come?" asked Bennet.

"You have school," said his mother.

"It's okay if I'm late," said Bennet.

"No, it's not okay," said his mother. "This is a big day for you."

She was right—it *was* a big day. It was the day of the mayoral debate. The two candidates who were running for mayor of North Agaming were coming to Bennet's school to debate the issues. Bennet was one of the kids who was going to be up onstage, asking the candidates questions.

"That's not until eleven o'clock," he said.

Mr. Ordway called out from the bathroom: "Get your stuff ready, Bennet. I'll drop you off at school."

Ten minutes later, Bennet and his father were on their way out to the garage. While Mr. Ordway went to push the button that operated the automatic garage-door opener, Bennet tossed his backpack into the backseat of Mr. Ordway's old Honda sedan.

"I'll go get Pete," said Bennet as he stepped out onto the driveway.

"Make it quick," said his father. "I'm in kind of a rush this morning."

Bennet hurried over to the house next door. It was unseasonably mild—it felt more like early September than mid-October. Bennet went around to the back, where the kitchen was located. Pete Nickowsky was Bennet's best friend. He and Bennet were practically inseparable.

Bennet peered in through the sliding glass door. A maple tree's red and orange leaves were reflected in the glass. Bennet saw Emma, Pete's older sister, at the kitchen table. Emma was a junior in high school. She was watching MTV while she ate an English muffin. Bennet didn't see Pete anywhere. He tapped on the glass.

Emma got up from the table and slid open the door. "Pete's out walking Gus," she said. Gus was Pete's black Labrador.

Bennet knew his father was in too much of a hurry to wait for Pete. "Could you tell Pete that my dad drove me to school?"

Emma said she would.

Mr. Ordway had backed the car out of the garage and was waiting behind the wheel, with the motor running, when Bennet returned.

"Where's Pete?" asked Mr. Ordway as Bennet hopped into the front seat. He started backing up the moment Bennet closed his door. He was listening to an all-news AM radio station. Mr. Ordway was a big news addict.

"He's out walking Gus," said Bennet.

Bennet said nothing on the way to school. He just looked out his window. The suburban landscape was a spectacular mix of orange and yellow and red trees.

"So," said Mr. Ordway, "have you figured out what you're going to ask the candidates at the debate this morning?"

"No," replied Bennet.

"Cutting it kind of close, aren't you?"

"Yeah," answered Bennet.

Bennet knew he wasn't being very communicative, but he didn't really feel much like talking. He was mad that he couldn't go with his father to Town Hall to see the pumpkin.

But then a surprising thing happened. When they got to Bennet's school, Mr. Ordway drove right past the long, flat-roofed brick building. At the next traffic light, he turned down Butler Street—which was the way to Town Hall.

Bennet, dumbfounded, stared at his father.

Mr. Ordway smiled and said, "Don't you dare tell your mother."

THE PRANK

Way I see it, this is an education, too," said Mr. Ordway as they drove to the Town Hall.

"I ag-g-gree with you," said Bennet.

"I mean, you can't learn *everything* in a class-room," said Mr. Ordway.

"That's what I say," said Bennet.

"Oh, for crying out loud," said Mr. Ordway, glancing at his rearview mirror.

Bennet swung around to take a look.

A large red pickup truck was tailgating them. The vehicle was following dangerously close. If Mr. Ordway were to stop suddenly, the truck would bash right into them. The driver was a big, hairy guy with a mustache and a baseball cap on his head.

"You fathead, stop tailgating!" cried Mr. Ord-way.

"L-l-let me handle this, Dad," said Bennet.

He reached under his seat and grabbed a com-

puter keyboard. It was Bennet's latest invention—
c-mail, he called it. The *c* stood for "car." Bennet
was always inventing things. He picked up the cord
that was attached to the beige keyboard and
plugged it into the car cigarette lighter. Then he
plugged in some wires that he had rigged up under
the dashboard.

Mr. Ordway glanced at Bennet and chuckled.
"You and your crazy inventions," he said.

Bennet tapped a message on the computer keyboard. He pressed the RETURN button. This sent
the message from the keyboard to a long, narrow
electronic sign that Bennet had rigged up in the
car's rear window. The sign relayed Bennet's message—in bright, licorice-red letters.

"*Whoa!*" exclaimed Mr. Ordway, peering into
his rearview mirror. "He sure backed off fast. What
did you say to him?"

"I wrote: 'You fathead! Stop tailgating!' "

"You didn't!" said Mr. Ordway, glancing at
Bennet.

"I d-did," said Bennet.

"You shouldn't have said that," said his father.

"But that's what *you* said."

"Yeah, but I never would say it to his face," said
Mr. Ordway.

"Well, it worked, d-didn't it?" said Bennet, grinning.

They turned down a residential street, then another, more commercial street. This put them directly across from Town Hall. A small crowd was gathered on the lawn in front of the old brick building. Many of the people had their heads tilted back as they gazed up at the tall flagpole that stood in front of the building.

But no flag was flying. Instead, an enormous pumpkin was sitting at the top of the flagpole.

It looked so weird.

Bennet's father broke out laughing. "Man, I wish I had stories like this to cover every day."

Mr. Ordway drove into the Town Hall parking lot and parked. Bennet slung his backpack over his shoulder and followed his father across the front lawn to the main entrance of the building. A police officer stood near the front steps beside a blue wooden sawhorse that said POLICE—DO NOT CROSS. The barricade had been set up to keep people from using the main entrance so nobody would get hurt if the pumpkin were to fall to the ground.

"You've done some pretty nutty things in your time, Frank," Mr. Ordway teased the police officer, "but this one takes the cake."

The police officer laughed. He had a cheerful smile, a booming laugh.

"This looks more like one of your pranks, Mr. Ordway . . . or should I say your son's." The policeman smiled at Bennet. He was one of the officers who had been on duty when Bennet and Pete had been arrested for the Deep Doo-Doo broadcasts.

"Bennet's mischief days are over—right, Ben?"

"Right, Dad," said Bennet.

"Any idea who did it?" Mr. Ordway asked the police officer.

"We don't have a clue," he replied. "The custodian discovered the pumpkin this morning when he got here. That's all we know."

Mr. Ordway went to look for the custodian. Bennet followed. They found him behind the building, sweeping up around a Dumpster.

The custodian was not terribly informative, though. In fact, he pretty much just repeated what the police officer had said.

While Mr. Ordway talked to the custodian, Bennet opened his backpack and took out his secondhand digital camera. He always carried his camera around in his backpack—he had gotten it on his last birthday so he could have it for situations like this. First, he took two shots of the pumpkin on the flag- · pole. Then he took a picture of the custodian.

Bennet returned the camera to his backpack and walked back to his father's car. He opened the door behind the driver's seat. His father's blue canvas brief bag was lying on the backseat. Bennet unzipped it and took out his father's cell phone. He punched in a phone number.

"Please, be there," muttered Bennet, pressing the SEND button.

As Bennet listened to the phone ring on the other end, he gazed up at the pumpkin perched on top of the flagpole. Someone had gone to a lot of trouble to put that pumpkin up there.

Why?

THE DEEP DOO-DOO WEB SITE

For someone who had to be at school in twenty minutes, Pete Nickowsky was sure taking his sweet time. First, he had two bowls of Cap'n Crunch. As he ate, he casually flipped through an entire L.L. Bean catalog. Then he put his cereal bowl in the kitchen sink and fed his black Labrador, Gus.

"Speak, Gus," said Pete as he stood in front of the dog, holding up a bowl of dog food.

The black Lab barked.

"Good dog!" said Pete, pleased. "Now lie down."

The dog lay down on the linoleum floor.

"Now give me your paw."

The dog gave him his paw.

"Now your other paw."

The dog, barking, obeyed.

Pete set the bowl down on the kitchen floor. He

was petting Gus on the head when the cordless phone on the kitchen counter rang—or, more precisely, bleated.

Pete picked up the phone and said, "Nickowsky's Morgue. You kill 'em, we chill 'em."

"Good, you're still there!" It was Bennet.

"Hey, what's the big idea of leaving without me?" demanded Pete. He and Bennet always went to school together.

"I got a ride with my dad," said Bennet. "He was in a rush."

"Where are you calling from?" asked Pete.

"I'm at Town Hall."

"Town Hall?" cried Pete. "What the heck are you doing *there?*"

"I'm covering a b-big story."

"You are? Without *me?*" said Pete. He was hurt and angry. What did Bennet know about covering a story? Nothing! Oh, sure, his father was a reporter for the local paper, but it was Pete, not Bennet, who liked to write. Bennet liked to invent things.

"I came by to get you, but you were out walking Gus," said Bennet. "Anyway, wait till you hear what's happened."

"What?" asked Pete, sulking.

"You know the flagpole in front of Town Hall?"

"What about it?"

"Well, get this: Someone stuck a pumpkin on top of it."

"Get out!"

"I'm serious!"

"Cool!" said Pete. "Who did it?"

"Nobody knows. Anyway, you've got to put the story up."

Pete stepped over to the refrigerator. He grabbed the notepad that was sticking to the front of the refrigerator. He selected a sharp pencil from the bouquet of pencils that sat in an old ceramic marmalade jar on the counter.

"Okay, Alva, what do you have?" he said. "Alva" was Pete's nickname for Bennet. He got the name from Thomas Edison. Alva was Thomas Edison's middle name.

"Someone stuck a pumpkin on the Town Hall flagpole last night."

"Details, Ordway, details! I want details!"

Bennet told him all the details he knew.

Then he said, "My dad's coming! Gotta go! See you at school!"

Pete hung up, ripped off the sheet of paper he had scribbled on, and hurried over to Bennet's house.

Although Pete was almost certain that Mrs. Ordway had left for the day, he rang the front doorbell just to make sure. When there was no answer, he peeked through the front hallway window. It was dark inside the house. Pete glanced about to make sure nobody was looking, then he jumped off the porch and into the rhododendron bushes that grew alongside the front of the house. The key to the Ordways' front door was hidden in a small fake rock near the drainpipe. Little did Mr. and Mrs. Ordway suspect that Pete knew all about the fake rock and where Mr. Ordway had carefully hidden it.

Pete opened the front door and let himself into the Ordways' house. He went into the kitchen, grabbed a doughnut, then went upstairs to Bennet's bedroom. He sat down at Bennet's desk and turned on his computer.

Pete clicked open the Web site that he and Bennet had created—the Deep Doo-Doo Web site.

The home page consisted of a big head shot of Pete's dog, Gus, wearing the Dracula mask that Gus had worn during the Deep Doo-Doo broadcasts. Bennet had built a transmitter that had enabled him and Pete to interrupt a local TV station. The broadcasts, which had caused something of a national sensation, had directly affected the outcome of the governor's race. The boys had chosen Gus for the home page because everybody knew

Gus from the broadcasts. As he looked straight at the viewer, Gus's tongue moved in and out of his mouth. It was one of Bennet's little Web programming tricks. Then the dog began winking. Another of Bennet's tricky animations. Bennet was a genius at stuff like that. The words "DEEP DOO-DOO" appeared on the screen, as colorful as a box of crayons. The letters arched over Gus's head. Then the letters began blinking on and off like a Las Vegas nightclub sign.

The home page had a section devoted to the latest news. Yesterday's lead story was that Josh Blackman, a boy in Pete and Bennet's grade, had been sent to the principal's office for blowing spitballs through a straw while he was in science class.

It had been a slow news day.

But not today! Pete wanted today's headline to be a real gem. Usually, he had to think long and hard about a headline. Today, though, the headline just popped into his head. Here's what he typed:

Oh, Say Can You See . . . A Pumpkin!

Pete proceeded to write the article. He didn't write much. There wasn't much to write.

SCOOPED!

After leaving Town Hall, Mr. Ordway drove Bennet to school. They got there just as the homeroom bell was ringing. Bennet grabbed his backpack and hopped out of the car.

"Thanks, Dad, for l-letting me come with you. That pumpkin was really cool."

"Glad you enjoyed it," said Mr. Ordway. "Well, see you at the debate." His father would be returning later that morning to cover the debate for *The Sun*.

Bennet dashed up the front steps and entered the school. Because he was one of the participants in the debate, Bennet didn't have to report to his homeroom. He was to report directly to the auditorium, where a rehearsal for the debate had been scheduled.

Ms. Jones, who ran the media center, was in charge of the rehearsal. She and Mr. O'Leary, who taught music, sat on stools in the center of the stage and pretended to be the mayoral candidates. Fifteen children, including Bennet, sat on folding chairs to the side of the stage and asked them questions. Ms. Jones took the rehearsal very seriously. But not Mr. O'Leary. He gave the funniest answers. When Bennet asked him how he felt about closing the town dump, Mr. O'Leary replied, "Hey, leave my car out of this."

Everyone laughed, even Ms. Jones.

At 10:30—a half hour before the mayoral debate was to begin—a few other kids began showing up in the auditorium. One of these kids was Pete. He was reporting the story for the Deep Doo-Doo Web site.

The rehearsal ended just as Pete came into the auditorium. Bennet hurried up the aisle to meet him.

"So how'd the story go?" he asked.

Pete gave Bennet a blank look. He seemed puzzled. "Story? What story?" he said. "Oh, my gosh, the *story!*" he cried, slapping his forehead.

"You didn't really forget, did you?"

Pete chuckled. "Of course I didn't forget," he said. "I'm just kidding you, Alva."

"Don't kid around like that," said Bennet. Then, breaking into a smile, he rubbed his hands together in glee. "I guess we scooped my dad's paper."

"I guess we did," said Pete, grinning fiendishly.

"We're good!" said Bennet.

"We're the best," said Pete.

"We're number o—"

"Hey, guys," said a girl's voice.

Bennet swung around and nearly smacked into Elizabeth Smith, who was also in the sixth grade.

Pete broke into a big, goofy grin. "Oh, hi, Elizabeth!" he said.

Pete had a huge crush on Elizabeth.

Bennet, who didn't, just said, "Hey."

Elizabeth was the editor-in-chief of *The Purple Patch*, the school newspaper. *The Purple Patch* covered many of the same stories that Bennet and Pete's Deep Doo-Doo Web site covered. In that respect, Bennet considered Elizabeth an arch rival. Unlike the Deep Doo-Doo Web site, though, *The Purple Patch* also printed crosswords and find-the-missing-words puzzles. The Deep Doo-Doo Web site would never, ever, print something as trivial as those.

"Ready for the mayoral debate?" Elizabeth asked. She was covering the story for *The Purple Patch*.

"Ready as we'll ever be," said Bennet.

"I think this is *so* exciting," she gushed.

"Yeah, real exciting," said Bennet.

"Why are you all dressed up?" asked Pete.

Bennet had been wondering the same thing. Usually, Elizabeth wore old overalls or baggy jeans to school. Today, though, she was dressed as though it were class-picture day. She had on a blue dress, and her shoulder-length blond hair was pulled back with a purple ribbon.

Elizabeth groaned. "It was my mom's idea. She said I had to get dressed up because I'm interviewing the candidates after the debate."

"You're *interviewing* the candidates?" said Bennet in astonishment. "How did you manage to swing that?"

"I asked," she replied.

Bennet gave Pete a look. He sure wished Pete would think to ask things like that.

"Well, good luck up there," she said to Bennet. "And good luck covering the story," she said to Pete.

"Hey, thanks!" said Pete happily.

Elizabeth turned to go, then stopped.

"Oh, I almost forgot," she said, pulling out some computer printouts from her notebook. The printouts, which were on purple paper, were held together by a big paper clip. "This is for you, and this is for you." She handed each boy a printout.

"What's this?" asked Pete.

"A *Purple Patch* news flash," replied Elizabeth. "Someone put a pumpkin on top of the Town Hall flagpole. Can you believe it?"

Bennet stared at the news flash. Then he stared at Elizabeth. He was incredulous. "H-h-how did you find out about this?"

"My father's a volunteer fireman," she replied. "The fire department was called out at six o'clock this morning to try and get the pumpkin down with the hook-and-ladder truck. It was so difficult to reach, though, they couldn't get it."

Bennet wondered if Elizabeth had scooped him and Pete on the pumpkin story. He knew Pete had posted their story at around 8:30.

Elizabeth said, "I got here at seven o'clock this morning to write the story so I could hand it out when kids started showing up at eight."

She had scooped them!

"Well, see ya," said Elizabeth. She turned and headed down the aisle to the first row.

Bennet was furious. He crunched up *The Purple Patch* news flash into a little ball and flung it into one of the rows.

THE DEBATE

At around twenty minutes to eleven, reporters and news photographers—including Bennet's father and a photographer from *The Sun*—began arriving in the auditorium to cover the debate. A short time later, the two men who were running for mayor—Mr. Robert J. Abbott and Mr. Bruce Johnson—showed up onstage in dark suits, smiling and shaking hands. Then the fifth- and sixth-grade classes trooped into the auditorium and sat down. A few minutes later, the candidates and the kids participating in the debate took their seats onstage. At 11:00, the mayoral debate began—right on schedule.

First, Ms. Henriquez, the principal, stood at the lectern and announced over the PA system how pleased she was that the debate was being held at the school. She turned to the two candidates onstage and thanked each one for coming. They, in turn, thanked Ms. Henriquez and all the students for inviting them.

Then Ms. Henriquez introduced Joel Fischer, who was to ask the first question.

"Where do you stand on funding for school sports programs?" asked Joel, speaking into a handheld microphone. It was funny to hear his voice booming throughout the entire auditorium.

Mr. Abbott spoke first. He was a tall, lanky man with a serious expression and wavy hair. "I used to play football in high school," he said, "so I know how important school sports programs are. I fully support them. What's more, I know our town parks are in bad shape. They need renovating. As your mayor, I will make fixing up our parks a top priority."

Mr. Johnson was a short, stocky man with little hair and a big smile. He waited for the applause to die down and then he said, "As a former catcher on my Little League baseball team, I, too, know how important sports are for kids. I'm all for them. In fact, my motto is: Do sports, not drugs."

"Thank you," said Joel over the applause, and sat down. He passed the microphone to Taisha Barnes, who was seated beside him.

Taisha stood, introduced herself, and asked the

candidates what role African-Americans would play in their administrations.

Both of them promised that African-Americans would play important roles.

Then Adam Resnick stood and introduced himself. He had his question printed on a piece of paper. "This question is for Mr. Abbott," he said. "Mr. Abbott, I've read in the newspaper that you're a hothead. Is this true?"

The auditorium instantly became very quiet. Nobody could believe Adam would ask such a thing.

But Mr. Abbott just laughed. "Yes, Adam, I read that article, too. I'm happy to tell you that, no, I'm not a hothead. What I am is very passionate about certain issues. Unfortunately, some people in the media tend to confuse passion with anger."

The audience started to clap when Mr. Johnson spoke up. "I just want to say that I'm every bit as passionate about issues, but nobody has ever accused me of being a hothead."

Now it was Bennet's turn. He glanced over at the front row, where the press sat. Bennet's father smiled at him. Pete gave him a big thumbs-up. Elizabeth's head was lowered as she busily jotted in her notebook.

Suddenly an idea popped into Bennet's head.

Sure, Elizabeth may have scooped them on the pumpkin story, but that didn't mean he and Pete couldn't take credit for it.

"Bennet?" said Ms. Henriquez. She made a face to indicate that everyone was waiting for him to speak.

Bennet stood, cleared his voice, and said:

"Hi, I'm Bennet Ordway. T-t-today, the lead story on the Deep Doo-Doo Web site is that a pumpkin was discovered on top of the Town Hall f-f-flagpole. I wonder if you'd like to comment on this?"

There, he had done it. He had stolen the scoop from Elizabeth. Now everyone would think he and Pete had reported the story first.

Mr. Johnson, chuckling, said, "Obviously, who-ever put it up there has a real sense of humor."

"This is where we part company," said Mr. Abbott, folding his arms and looking deadly serious. "Personally, I'm outraged that someone would do such a thing."

Mr. Johnson turned to Mr. Abbott and said, "Oh, come on, Bob, it's just a prank."

Mr. Abbott shook his head. He gave the audience a "can you believe this guy?" look. Then, turning to Mr. Johnson, he said, "You call it a prank? I call it disrespectful of town property. This city needs a mayor who knows the difference between what's right and wrong. As I've said again and again during this campaign, if I'm elected mayor, I promise to set a good example for today's youth."

Bennet thanked the two candidates. He handed the microphone to Franny Singer beside him and plunked down into his chair.

Bennet could feel his whole body trembling. It always made him nervous to speak in front of a lot of people. But that was only part of the reason why he was trembling so much. He was also nervous about Elizabeth. He knew—even without glancing over at her—that she was mad at him for stealing her scoop.

He could *feel* her scorching glare.

YOU CAN'T DO THAT!

When the debate was over, Bennet didn't hang around to shake hands with the candidates the way the other students onstage did. He disappeared backstage and slipped out the door that led to the cafeteria. Pete must have known that's what Bennet would do, for he was outside the door, waiting.

"Hey, nice job, Alva," said Pete. He gave Bennet a big hearty pat on the back.

"Thanks," said Bennet.

"I've got to tell you, though," said Pete as they began walking to their classrooms. "I was kind of surprised you took credit for the pumpkin story."

"I d-d-didn't exactly take credit for it," said Bennet.

Pete gave him a look.

"Okay, m-m-maybe I did," admitted Bennet. "But w-w-we don't know for sure she reported the story before us."

"Did you see Elizabeth's face?" asked Pete. The hall was now mobbed with kids returning to their classes.

"No," said Bennet. "Why? D-d-did she look mad?"

"Mad as a hornet," said Pete.

"Well, too bad for her," said Bennet.

While Bennet may have sounded like he couldn't care less if Elizabeth was annoyed at him, he did care. He cared plenty. In fact, he went out of his way to avoid Elizabeth. He kept a sharp eye out for her wherever he went. He did a good job of not bumping into her—that is, until Mr. Vreeland's 2:00 social-studies class. Elizabeth's desk was right beside Bennet's. She was seated at her desk when Bennet walked into the room.

Fortunately, Pete was in the class, too. He would be there to give Bennet moral support.

"Well, good luck," said Pete. He gave Bennet a playful punch on the arm, and then walked over and sat down at his desk—way over by the tall windows at the other side of the classroom.

Bennet sighed as he took his seat. He expected Elizabeth to light into him. But she didn't. In fact, she didn't say a word. She didn't even glance over at him.

Mr. Vreeland began class by talking about the

debate. Then he turned his attention—and the class's—to the lesson he had planned for that day.

"For the past month," he said, "we've been studying the Civil War. Today we're going to break up into teams of two students each and begin doing projects on the Civil War."

As Bennet was listening to Mr. Vreeland, he heard Elizabeth whisper: "I hate you!"

Bennet pretended he didn't hear.

"Now, your projects can be about anything on the Civil War," said Mr. Vreeland.

"How could you do such a thing?" whispered Elizabeth.

"Do what?" asked Bennet innocently, glancing over at her.

Up at the front of the classroom, Mr. Vreeland said, "Is there something you wish to share with the rest of the class, Mr. Ordway?"

Everyone turned in their seats and stared curiously at Bennet.

Bennet felt his face burn with embarrassment. "Uh, n-n-no," he replied.

"You sure?" said Mr. Vreeland.

"Yes," said Bennet.

"If it isn't asking too much, Mr. Ordway, I'd like to have your undivided attention, please."

"Yes, Mr. Vreeland," said Bennet.

"Now," said Mr. Vreeland, continuing, "I want these projects to be imaginative. In fact, the more imaginative, the better."

"You jerk!" said Elizabeth.

"I'm n-n-not a jerk," said Bennet.

"Mr. Ordway, you aren't talking in class again, are you?" asked Mr. Vreeland. He had the most incredulous expression on his face.

Once again, Bennet felt twenty-two pairs of eyes fixed on him. Twenty-three—he forgot Mr. Vreeland.

"N-n-no."

"*No?*"

"Yes."

"What is it? Yes or no?"

"Y-yes."

"Who, may I ask, were you talking to?"

"N-nobody."

"*Nobody?*" said Mr. Vreeland, arching an eyebrow. "You mean, you were talking to yourself?"

Bennet heard some giggles.

"N-n-no," he said.

"Well, then, who were you talking to?"

Bennet didn't know what to say. He didn't want to rat on Elizabeth. But what else could he do?

"I was talking to Elizabeth," said Bennet. "Sh-she keeps whispering to me."

"He stole my story!" blurted Elizabeth.

"We reported it f-first," protested Bennet.

"You did not!"

"We did, too!"

"You did not!"

"Children, please!" cried Mr. Vreeland. "Honestly!" He shook his head as if he couldn't believe such a disruption was actually happening in his classroom.

When he had complete silence, Mr. Vreeland said, "I was going to let everyone in the class pick whom he or she wanted to work with, but I've changed my mind. *I'm* going to decide who works with whom."

The whole class groaned. Michael Frierson swung around in his chair and glowered at Bennet.

"I'll start with Mr. Ordway and Miss Smith," said Mr. Vreeland. "Since the two of you have so much to say to each other, I want you two to work together—as a *team*."

"No!" cried Elizabeth.

"Y-y-you can't do that!" declared Bennet.

"I just did," replied Mr. Vreeland, and smiled.

A $500 PRIZE

That afternoon after school, like every afternoon after school, Bennet and Pete walked home together. "You are *so* lucky," said Pete as they walked along the sidewalk under a canopy of autumn-colored leaves. Both boys had their sweatshirts wrapped around their waists. Bennet, as usual, had on his Boston Red Sox cap. As usual, he had it stylishly flipped backward. "You get to do your project with Elizabeth. Man, I got stuck with boring old Natalie Phillips."

"Hey, I'd rather work with Natalie any day," said Bennet.

"We're doing our project on the Underground Railroad," said Pete. "What did you guys pick?"

"We haven't."

"You haven't?"

Bennet sighed. "We can't agree on anything."

"But—"

"I know. I know," said Bennet. "Mr. Vreeland said he wants to know what we're doing our projects on by the next time we meet. But what can I do? Elizabeth won't agree to anything. I asked her if she wanted to do our project on Harriet Tubman. No, she said. How about John Brown? No, she said. Abraham Lincoln? No."

"Wow, you *do* have a problem," said Pete.

The first thing Bennet and Pete always did after school was to go into Pete's house and feed Gus and let him out of the house. Then they went next door to Bennet's house to feed themselves. Today they had honey graham crackers and tall glasses of milk. Feeling the need for a little extra nourishment, Pete also opened up a can of large pitted black olives. Then the two boys went upstairs to Bennet's bedroom to update their Web site. Bennet was anxious to sit down at the computer and download the pumpkin photographs he had taken with his digital camera. Pete was anxious to write an article about the mayoral debate.

While Pete sat on Bennet's bed and wrote, Bennet turned on his computer. The first photo he downloaded was the one that showed the pumpkin way up on the flagpole. He showed the image to Pete.

"What a hoot!" cried Pete, laughing.

Bennet, smiling, placed the image above the headline that Pete had written that morning:

Oh, Say Can You See . . . A Pumpkin!

"So what do you think?" asked Bennet.

Pete took a look. "That is one great headline, if I do say so myself," said Pete.

"I mean, what do you think of where I placed the photograph?"

"Not bad," replied Pete. "I think my headline needs to be bigger, though."

"It's f-fine the size it is," said Bennet.

"Okay, Ordway, shove off. It's my turn to work at the computer," said Pete. "I have a debate to report on."

Bennet surrendered his chair to Pete. He stood and watched as Pete typed his headline.

" 'Abbott Wins D-d-debate,' " said Bennet, reading the headline aloud. "You really think he won?"

"Hey, anyone who says he's going to fix up our parks gets my vote," said Pete. "Besides, this town needs a no-nonsense guy like Abbott to keep people from putting pumpkins up on flagpoles."

That was Pete for you. Always kidding. Bennet,

smiling, heard the phone ring. He went into his parents' bedroom and picked up the phone by the bed and said, "Hello?"

"Hi, Ben," said Mr. Ordway on the other end. "You did great at the debate this morning."

"Thanks," replied Bennet.

"Mom home yet?" asked his father.

"N-not yet."

"Well, I'm just about to head home. Anything going on?"

"No," replied Bennet. "Any new developments on the pumpkin?"

"Nothing," replied Mr. Ordway. "Nobody has a clue who did it. It's become a big story, though. Everyone's covering it. A few reporters didn't even show up at the debate. I heard that there was even a reporter from *The New York Times* in town asking about it. And our newspaper is offering a five-hundred-dollar prize for anyone who solves it."

"Five hundred dollars!" said Bennet.

"Yeah. 'Course I don't suppose I should be telling you this before we run the article in tomorrow's paper. Knowing you, I'm sure you'll put it up on your Web site."

"Who *me*?"

Mr. Ordway chuckled. "I'll see you later."

The second Bennet hung up the phone, he

darted into his bedroom and cried: "I have another article for you to write."

"Hey, take a look at this e-mail," said Pete. While Bennet had been on the phone, Pete had gone on-line to check their Web site's e-mail messages. "Talk about weird e-mails," said Pete. "Listen to this. . . ."

Pete read the message aloud:

"Is it you or is it I?
It's so hard to think
When you've got a black eye.
Does anyone really know?
The old barn owl cries who, who, who's
That lurking in the shadows behind
The red tractor? Is it the . . .
Nope, it's just a pumpkin.
Some mystery!"

"What kind of an e-mail is *that*?" asked Bennet.

"A poet must've sent it to us," said Pete.

"A *bad* poet," said Bennet.

"It is pretty bad," Pete admitted.

"Why would someone send it to us?"

"The person is probably hoping we'll publish it on our Web site," said Pete.

"*Us?*" said Bennet.

"It's such bad poem, I doubt any other site will have anything to do with it."

"Well, f-f-forget it," said Bennet. "We're not that kind of a Web site. Now, c'mon, we have work to do. *The Sun* is offering a five-hundred-dollar prize to anyone who finds out who put the pumpkin on the Town Hall flagpole. If we f-f-figure it out, we'll win the prize—plus we'll scoop my dad's paper, not to mention *The P-Purple Patch.*"

SCENE OF THE CRIME

Pete grabbed a pad and pencil. "Okay," he said. "Let's write down everything we know."

"Well," said Bennet, "we know that the pumpkin was put on top of the f-flagpole by someone in the middle of the night."

"Which means the person must be an expert climber," said Pete. "Can you imagine climbing up a flagpole in the pitch dark?"

"And with a pumpkin," said Bennet.

"What else do we know?" asked Pete.

They thought for a long time, but neither one of them could think of anything else.

Bennet, frustrated, sighed. "The truth is," he said, "we know squat about who did it."

"Well, then, I'll tell you what we need to do," said Pete, putting down his pad and pencil. "We need to pay a visit to the scene of the crime and do some serious investigating."

• • •

They went the next afternoon. They got Pete's sister, Emma, to drive them. Emma, who had turned sixteen back in June, had recently acquired her driver's license. She drove them in the Nickowsky family's station wagon. She drove at the speed limit, and not one mph above.

"You drive like an old lady!" cried Pete. He was sitting in the backseat with Bennet. Emma refused to let either boy sit up front with her. The reason: passenger-side air bag.

"I do not drive like an old lady," protested Emma as she drove along Route 27, a four-lane road.

"I could walk faster than this," grumbled Pete.

"Then get out and walk," said Emma.

A green VW Jetta sped past them in the next lane. The car pulled in front of them. Apparently, it was too close for Emma's liking—she blasted her horn.

"What are you honking for?" asked Pete.

"I'm just driving defensively," replied Emma. "That's how I was taught to drive in driver's ed."

Pete had taken Gus with them. The black Lab was in the rear of the car, facing forward, with his head hanging over the backseat—just inches from Bennet's head. He was practically breathing in Bennet's face. Dog's breath! Bennet pushed Gus's head away. It was no use. The dog thought Bennet wanted his ear licked.

Another car passed them, a rusty old silver Toyota that looked like it was about to fall apart.

"Everyone's passing us!" complained Pete.

The Nickowskys' station wagon, like Mr. Ordway's car, was equipped with c-mail. Pete, being an aspiring writer, liked writing messages to other cars. Particularly cars that had pretty girls in them. Pete pointed to the keyboard that was on the floor by Bennet's feet.

"Hand me that keyboard, will ya?" he said.

Bennet gave it to him. Pete undid his seat belt and leaned forward into the front of the car.

"Don't mind me," he said to Emma as, hanging over the front passenger seat, he attached the keyboard's cord to the cigarette lighter and then connected some other wires that were dangling under the dashboard.

"In driver's ed I learned that most accidents happen within fifteen minutes from home," said Emma, with a disapproving look at Pete. "I'm sure it's because of things like *this*."

Pete sat back in his seat, buckled his seat belt, and began typing a message.

"What are you writing?" asked Emma, glancing in her rearview mirror.

"You mean what did I write?" said Pete as he sent his message. "I wrote: 'Honk if you think I drive too slow.' "

Just then, a black Nissan Pathfinder came up in the lane beside them. The guy at the wheel honked his horn. He looked over at Emma and laughed.

"You jerk!" Emma said to Pete. "Get rid of that message *now*!"

"Temper, temper!" said Pete.

"Peter Eric Nickowsky, you get rid of that message this instant!"

"Okay! Okay!" said Pete, chuckling. He deleted the message and handed the keyboard back to Bennet. "Gee whiz, a guy can't even have any fun."

It took them long enough, but they finally arrived at Town Hall. After Emma parked in the parking lot, they all got out of the car to look at the pumpkin on the flagpole.

Pete placed his right hand over his heart. "I pledge allegiance to the pumpkin of the United States of America."

Bennet laughed. Emma laughed, too, even though she was still annoyed at Pete.

Emma stayed outside with Gus while Bennet and Pete entered the building to find the custodian. They walked up one hall then down another, peeking into all the offices. They finally found the bald-

43

headed custodian in a large corner office, emptying a wastebasket.

"We'd like to ask you a few questions about the pumpkin," said Pete.

"Sorry, no questions," said the custodian as he put a new plastic liner in a metal wastebasket.

"But w-w-we just want to ask you a couple of things," Bennet said. "That's all."

"That's what that girl who was here earlier said," replied the custodian.

"A girl was here?" asked Pete.

"She said, 'I only have a couple of questions to ask you.' Next thing I knew she had taken out a little notebook and was asking me a million questions."

"Th-this girl," said Bennet. "She didn't have blond hair, did she?"

"Oh, so *you* know her!" said the custodian. "Cute girl." He gave Bennet a wink.

"Wh-wh-what did you tell her?" asked Bennet.

"Same thing I'll tell you," said the custodian. "I don't know anything about the pumpkin. I came into work one morning and there it was up on the flagpole. That's it. That's all I know," he said.

On the car ride back, Bennet hardly said a word, he was so upset. He couldn't believe that Elizabeth was also trying to solve the pumpkin mystery. She must have read about the $500 prize. But *The Purple Patch* didn't solve mysteries. *The Purple Patch* printed crosswords and find-the-hidden-words puzzles and stuff like that.

Bennet shuddered to think what would happen if Elizabeth solved the mystery.

What a catastrophe that would be!

When they got back to the Nickowskys' driveway, Bennet just wanted to go home, plop himself down in front of the TV, and forget today ever happened.

But Pete had other ideas. He wanted to come over and write a story about their trip to Town Hall and post it on the Web site. Bennet tried to talk him out of it, but Pete would not listen.

"There's nothing to write about," said Bennet as he and Pete entered his bedroom. He flicked on the lamp that was on his dresser.

"What do you mean there's nothing to write about?" Pete said as he pressed the button to start the computer. "What about the custodian? As far as I'm concerned, he's our number-one suspect."

"But he doesn't know a thing," said Bennet.

"So he says," said Pete.

"Well, I believe him," said Bennet.

Several clicks of the mouse later, Pete was online. "Oh, no!" he cried. "Not another poem!"

"We got *another* one?" said Bennet.

"This poem is even worse than the last," groaned Pete. "Listen:

More words begin with the letter R
Than with the letter U,
But not many people are interested.
All they care about is getting in
to a school of higher learning.
Oh, my!
I just love a good secret!
Here's one: my faith in you is as strong as iron ore.
I think not!"

"Even *I* can write better poetry than this," said Bennet. "It doesn't even make sense."

"Maybe the person's mad," said Pete.

"Mad?"

"Yeah, you know, like insane."

"Oh, great, that's all we need," said Bennet. "An insane poet sending us poems."

"It's from somebody who calls himself *hotstuff* in his e-mail address," Pete said.

"That could be anybody. Well, wh-whatever you do," said Bennet, "don't write back. We don't want to encourage the person."

"Particularly somebody who calls himself *hot-stuff.*"

Bennet groaned. What a horrible afternoon it had been! First, they had found out that Elizabeth was trying to solve the pumpkin mystery. Now a mad poet had sent them another awful poem.

What next?

WORST THING IN THE WORLD

What seems to be the problem here?"

Bennet stood in front of Mr. Vreeland's desk, staring down at his sneakers. His heart was thumping. He didn't know what to say. He was hoping that Elizabeth, who was standing beside him, would say something. After all, it was *her* fault that Mr. Vreeland was making them stay after class.

But Elizabeth didn't say a word.

Mr. Vreeland sat at his desk, waiting for a response. "Bennet? Elizabeth?" he said.

Finally, Elizabeth spoke. "We can't agree on a topic, Mr. Vreeland."

Bennet blew his top. He turned and glared at Elizabeth. "Excuse me?" he cried. "*We* can't agree? Y-y-you mean *you*! I c-can agree! It's *you* who c-c-can't agree!"

"I can so agree!" protested Elizabeth.

"You can not!" shot back Bennet.

"Can so!"

"Can not!"

Mr. Vreeland made a time-out signal with his hands.

"Children, *please!*" he said. "My goodness! Since the two of you obviously cannot agree on a topic, I'll just have to choose one for you. Let's see . . ." He thought for a minute. "Okay, I've got a topic," he said. "I want you to write about what factors led to the Civil War."

Bennet and Elizabeth turned to leave.

"That's funny," said Mr. Vreeland. "I don't recall hearing myself say you could leave."

Bennet and Elizabeth turned and came back.

"I thought you should know that, due to your bickering, I'm automatically giving you both a lower mark on this project," Mr. Vreeland said.

Bennet groaned. He felt like throttling Elizabeth. He suddenly knew what his next invention was going to be: an anti–Elizabeth Smith device! A loud alarm would go off whenever she was within fifty yards, warning the person.

"There is, however," continued Mr. Vreeland, "one thing you can do to help your grade—which I strongly recommend you do. In fact, you'll not only raise your mark, you'll also learn something about the Civil War."

"What's that?" asked Bennet.

"I've been reading both *The Purple Patch* and the Deep Doo-Doo Web site. I know that you're both trying to solve the Town Hall pumpkin mystery. So here's what I'd like you to do: I'd like you to work *together* to try to solve the mystery of who put the pumpkin on top of the flagpole."

"*What!*" gasped Bennet.

"What's *that* got to do with the Civil War?" asked Elizabeth.

"On the surface, nothing," replied Mr. Vreeland. "However, like yourselves, neither the North nor the South could work things out. So they went to war. You two can show me how well you can work things out together. You can show me how well you can work together on solving this mystery—without going to war."

"That's not fair!" cried Bennet.

"No, it's not!" said Elizabeth.

"See that?" said Mr. Vreeland, pleased. "The two of you are already agreeing."

"Really, Mr. Vreeland, isn't there something else we can do to raise our mark?" asked Bennet.

"Sorry," said Mr. Vreeland, shaking his head.

"It's either work together on the pumpkin mystery or get a lower mark."

Bennet and Elizabeth glanced at each other. Bennet gave a little sigh and said, "I guess w-we can work together."

Mr. Vreeland smiled. "*That's* what I like to hear: teamwork!"

TWO BRAINSTORMS IN ONE DAY

"You're sure she's cool about this?" asked Pete the next day at lunch. He sounded very nervous.

"Yes, I'm sure," replied Bennet, who wasn't the least bit nervous. He popped a French fry into his mouth.

Pete needed further assurance. "Elizabeth really said she didn't mind me being here?" he asked.

"Here" was the school cafeteria. Bennet and Elizabeth had arranged to meet at lunch so they could go over what each knew about the Town Hall pumpkin.

"I d-d-didn't give her a choice," said Bennet. "I told her the Deep Doo-Doo Web site belongs to me and you. Whatever involves me, involves you."

Bennet thought Pete would, at the very least, thank him for including him. But he didn't. Instead, Pete held up his spoon and inspected his reflection in the concave surface. He smoothed his long dirty-blond hair with his fingertips.

"How do I look?" he asked.

"You l-l-look fine," Bennet replied. He dipped another French fry into a puddle of ketchup on his plate. Pete hadn't touched his lunch. He was too anxious about meeting with Elizabeth.

"You didn't even look at me!" said Pete.

Bennet rolled his eyes. As he turned to give Pete his *full* attention, he spotted Elizabeth, tray in hand, coming toward them.

"Here she is," said Bennet.

Pete, whirling about, leaped to his feet. "Well, hi, Elizabeth!" he said. Smiling, he pulled a chair out for her.

Elizabeth was not in a good mood. She didn't even smile or thank Pete. She set her tray on the table and sat down. A little spiral-bound notebook was on her tray next to her plate.

Elizabeth got right to business. "So what do you have so far on the pumpkin?"

"Wh-wh-what do *you* have?" asked Bennet.

"No, you first," said Elizabeth.

"N-n-no, no, no, you first," insisted Bennet.

"Fine," said Elizabeth. She picked up her notebook and flipped it open. "Let's see . . ." she said, reading her notes. She looked up. "Here's what I figure." She held up her index finger. "One, it's got to be a mountain climber or a window washer or someone who's an expert at climbing."

"That's what we figure, too," said Pete as, folding his arms on the table, he leaned forward. He looked terribly earnest.

Elizabeth held up another finger. "Two, it's dangerous climbing up a flagpole. That means it has to be more than just a prank."

"Excellent point!" said Pete. "Really excellent!"

"Do you have any s-s-suspects?" asked Bennet.

"Yeah, you guys," said Elizabeth.

"Us!" cried Bennet and Pete, glancing at each other in disbelief.

"You're the ones who did the Deep Doo-Doo broadcasts. It'd be just like you to pull a stunt like this."

"Well, it isn't us!" said Bennet indignantly.

"Your turn," said Elizabeth. "What do you have so far?"

Bennet told her that they, too, knew the person had to be an expert climber. "We also know it was done during the night," he said.

Elizabeth did not look impressed.

"That's it?" she said. "I thought you would have more than that."

"Well, it's a lot more than what *you* have," replied Bennet.

"It is not," said Elizabeth.

"It is, too," said Bennet.

"It is not."

"Is, too."

"Oh, my gosh!" cried Pete.

Bennet and Elizabeth stopped squabbling and looked at Pete.

"What's *your* problem?" asked Elizabeth.

Pete sank down in his chair. "Natalie Phillips is heading this way!" he wailed.

Sure enough, she was. She was with her best friend, Ingrid Saunders. The two of them were walking straight toward the empty table that was behind Elizabeth.

"Yeah? So?" said Elizabeth.

"She wanted to work with me on our project during lunch," said Pete. He was now all the way underneath the table. "If she catches me working with you guys, I'm dead meat."

"Oh, you poor thing," said Elizabeth. She sounded very sarcastic.

Pete looked frantically up at Bennet. "You gotta help me, Alva."

"*Alva?*" said Elizabeth, peering at Bennet.

"Yeah, as in Thomas Alva Edison," replied

Bennet. "I don't suppose you've ever heard of him."

"I've heard of him," said Elizabeth.

"C'mon, Bennet, help me!" said Pete.

"Wh-what can I do?" asked Bennet.

"You gotta get her attention so I can sneak out of here."

"How are you going to do that, *Alvie*?" asked Elizabeth. She was relishing every moment of this, Bennet could tell.

"I don't know," he said. He did know this: He hated Elizabeth Smith's guts.

"Hey, I know what you could do," said Elizabeth. "You could surprise Natalie by giving her a big kiss on the cheek. *That* would sure get her attention."

Bennet was not amused. "Very funny," he said.

"You're probably too scared to do something like that," said Elizabeth.

"I am not!"

"I bet you are."

"Well, you're wrong," said Bennet.

"Then why don't you do it?"

"Because I know of something better I can do," said Bennet.

"Oh?" Elizabeth said. "Like what?"

"You'll see," replied Bennet.

"Well, you better hurry up and do it," said Elizabeth. "She's here."

So she was. Natalie and Ingrid set their trays down on the next table. Natalie, who was very thin, had nothing but vegetables on her plate. Natalie never ate anything that was greasy or unhealthy for her. Back in elementary school, while all the other kids brought in things like Cheez Doodles and Oreos for snack time, she brought in baby carrots.

"All right, here I go," said Bennet. He stood, picked up his tray, and marched out into the middle of the cafeteria.

There was just one problem: he had no idea what he was going to do.

Then he had a brainstorm.

Bennet stopped and closed his eyes. Just thinking about what he was about to do next made his hands tremble, his knees grow wobbly.

Well, here goes nothing, he thought. With that, he let go of his tray.

The tray hit the cafeteria floor with a tremendous crash. Ketchup splattered. Silverware clattered. A small, empty chocolate-pudding bowl rolled noisily across the floor, vanishing under a table.

It was as if a firecracker had exploded. Everyone in the cafeteria stopped what they were doing and turned and stared at Bennet. Nobody moved a muscle.

Nobody, that is, except Pete. He stole past Natalie, without her even noticing. In a flash, he was across the cafeteria. Before he stepped out, Pete stopped, turned, put his hands together in prayer, and bowed to Bennet. Then he disappeared out the door.

Only two kids noticed Pete leave: Bennet and Elizabeth.

That's when Bennet had his second brainstorm.

Could the pumpkin be a cover-up?

A DEEP, DARK SECRET

A *cover-up?*" said Pete later that day in the Ordways' kitchen. He and Bennet were sitting at the kitchen table, snacking on pretzel sticks and milk.

"I thought of it t-t-today," said Bennet. "You know, in the cafeteria. It occurred to me that m-maybe someone put the pumpkin on top of the flagpole to take everyone's attention away from something else. You know, to hide some deep, dark secret."

"Such as?" asked Pete, biting off the tip of a pretzel stick.

"Well, that's what I'm not sure about," replied Bennet. He opened the newspaper that was lying on the kitchen table between them. The first thing Bennet had done when he arrived home from school was to retrieve the newspaper from the blue recycling bin out in the garage. "That's why I wanted this n-n-newspaper. It's the paper that came out the day before the pumpkin appeared. I figure something must've happened that day which caused the person to climb the f-flagpole that night."

Pete reached for Section B of the newspaper. "Well, if you're right," he said, flipping it open, "it'll be in the police blotter."

"Why there?" asked Bennet.

"Because that's where all the juicy stuff appears," said Pete. "Let's see now . . ." He studied the police blotter. "A Craig Flynn of thirty-eight Putnam Street was arrested for disorderly conduct. A Diane Thompson of forty-nine Edgemont Lane was arrested for driving while under the influence of alcohol. A Mark Evans of one-seventeen Hamilton Street was also arrested for disorderly conduct following a family dispute." Pete looked up at Bennet. "Anything sound promising to you?"

"Not especially," Bennet started to say when the doorbell rang.

"Who could that be?" asked Pete.

"Probably Elizabeth," said Bennet, rising from his chair.

Pete spat out the pretzel stick he was chewing. He sprang to his feet, his eyes wide open.

"*Who?*" he cried.

60

"Elizabeth," said Bennet. "I invited her over so we c-c-could work on our project."

Pete rushed to the kitchen window and, lifting the curtain, peeked out. "Why didn't you tell me she was coming?"

"Because I knew if I did, y-y-you'd get all wigged out," said Bennet.

"I would not!" Pete said resentfully. "How do I look?"

"You look the way you always look," said Bennet.

Pete followed Bennet out into the front hallway. Bennet was about to open the door when Pete grabbed his arm, saying, "Wait! How's my breath smell?"

He breathed into Bennet's face.

"It smells pretzely," said Bennet.

"I better use mouthwash," said Pete, and dashed up the stairs.

Bennet rolled his eyes, sighed, and opened the front door. Elizabeth stood on the porch in a navy-blue sweatshirt that said WELLFLEET in big, happy, summery yellow letters across the front. Gus was at her side. Whenever Pete was at Bennet's, Gus came, too, and hung around outside the house.

"Let me guess," said Elizabeth as, bending, she patted Gus on the head. "This is the famous Deep Doo-Doo dog."

"That's him," said Bennet. He was holding the door open for Elizabeth when Gus darted inside.

"Gus!" shouted Bennet.

Tail wagging, Gus raced into the kitchen, sniffing at everything. Bennet hurried after him. Gus jumped up and put his front paws on the kitchen table and began sniffing the bag of pretzel sticks. Bennet grabbed him by the collar and yanked him away.

"Bad dog!" he said. He put Gus outside.

"Pete here?" asked Elizabeth, glancing about the kitchen.

"He's upstairs," said Bennet. "He'll be down in a minute. You want a pretzel or anything?"

Elizabeth glanced at the bag of pretzels that Gus's nose had just been in. "No thanks," she said. "So what's this great idea you wanted to tell me?"

Bennet sighed. Earlier that afternoon, as school was about to let out, he had boasted to Elizabeth that he knew how to figure out who was responsible for the pumpkin. Now he had to tell her that his great idea was a dud.

"I th-thought it might be a cover-up," he said.

He expected Elizabeth to laugh or make some sarcastic remark. But she didn't.

"A cover-up?" she said. "Hmm, interesting."

"Well, it would be a lot more interesting," replied Bennet, "if there was something in the n-n-newspaper that sounded like a cover-up, but there isn't."

Elizabeth picked up the front page of the newspaper. She studied it for a moment. "Well, no wonder," she said. "You're looking at the wrong newspaper."

"What's wrong about it?"

"Well," she replied, "the pumpkin appeared on top of the flagpole on the morning of October twelfth. The date of this newspaper is October eleventh. If something happened on the eleventh, it wouldn't appear in that day's paper. It would appear in the *next* day's paper. It always kills me when people buy an old newspaper of the day they were born. If they really want to see what happened on the day they were born, they should buy the *next* day's paper."

Much as Bennet hated to admit it, he knew Elizabeth was right. "I'll be right back," he said.

He went out to the recycling bin in the garage and got the newspaper that was dated October 12.

He came back inside and unfolded the paper on the kitchen table. As Elizabeth stood beside him, he flipped from one page to the next, looking for an article, any article, that seemed the least bit unusual.

"Well, hi, Elizabeth!" a loud, cheerful voice blurted out behind them.

Pete stood in the doorway, with a big, foolish grin on his face. While in the bathroom, he had wet and combed his hair. He came over to the table. His breath smelled like fresh mint. "Don't tell me you're still looking for a cover-up," he said to Bennet.

"We're looking in a different newspaper," said Bennet.

"Well, I told you where to look," said Pete. "The police blotter." He opened up Section B.

"Hey!" he cried.

"Hey what?" asked Bennet.

"Hey, listen to this," said Pete. "Robert Abbott of fifty-three Pine Drive reported that a twenty-one-speed Trek bicycle and some old record albums were stolen from his garage."

"You mean Robert Abbott the candidate for mayor?" asked Bennet.

"Let me see that," Elizabeth said. She practically ripped the newspaper out of Pete's hands. "It's him, all right," she said. "That's his address! I know because when I interviewed him after the debate, I asked him where he lived."

"Gee, I'm surprised he didn't say anything about the burglary during the debate," said Pete.

"Why would he say anything about it?" asked Elizabeth.

"Well, if *my* bike or tunes had been stolen, *I'd* sure say something," said Pete. "Particularly since the press was there. Think how hard the police would look for the crook if the burglary was plastered all over the papers."

"Plus it would be a good way to get votes," said Bennet. "People would feel s-sorry for him."

Elizabeth sat down. She helped herself to a pretzel stick from the bag on the table. "*This* is getting interesting," she said. "Hey, you got any milk?"

THE MAD POET

They spent the next half hour or so at the kitchen table, trying to figure out why Mr. Abbott didn't mention anything about the burglary during the debate—or afterward during his interview with Elizabeth.

"M-maybe he was nervous," suggested Bennet at one point.

"Nervous?" said Elizabeth.

"About having to debate," explained Bennet. "I know I get nervous when I'm in front of a lot of people."

"He didn't seem very nervous to me," said Pete.

"Nor me," said Elizabeth.

"Well, it was just a suggestion," said Bennet.

At twenty minutes to five, Mrs. Ordway walked into the kitchen. She was carrying two plastic bags of groceries. She took one look at Elizabeth seated at her kitchen table and did a double take. It wasn't every day Mrs. Ordway came home and found a girl in her kitchen.

"Well, hello!" she said as, smiling, she set her bags down on the kitchen counter.

"Hey, Mom," said Bennet. "This is El-l-lizabeth. Elizabeth, this is my mom."

"Hi," said Elizabeth.

"Nice to meet you," said Mrs. Ordway.

"W-w-we're doing a project together for school," said Bennet.

"What's the project?" asked his mother.

"Just a project," replied Bennet.

"So you're in Bennet's class?" Mrs. Ordway asked.

"Yes," said Elizabeth.

Bennet could see where things were heading. His mother was going to start asking Elizabeth questions. It wouldn't be just one or two questions. It would be a hundred million questions.

"W-w-we don't want to disturb you," Bennet told his mother. "We'll go up to my bedroom and work."

Once they were upstairs, Pete gave Elizabeth a mini-tour of the house. "This is the bedroom hallway," he said. "And this is a photograph of Alva when he was a little kid—what a cutie-pie, huh? . . . And this is Mr. and Mrs. Ordway's bedroom. . . . And this is the bathroom that Alva uses. . . . And this is his Scooby-Doo toothbrush." Pete got to Bennet's bedroom door and stopped. "And this," he announced, "is Alva's bedroom."

Pete flung open the door and snapped on the lamp on Bennet's dresser. "Careful where you step: it's a little messy."

It was more than just a little messy. Bennet's bed was unmade; he had books piled up high on his desk; his wastebasket was overflowing; and his clothes were tossed about all over the place—including his dirty underwear, which was lying right smack in the middle of the floor.

Bennet hurried over and kicked the underwear underneath the bed.

Pete sat down at Bennet's desk and turned on the computer. "And this is where we create the Deep Doo-Doo Web site," he said.

"Oh, no!" he groaned when, a few moments later, he was on-line. "Another e-mail from the Mad Poet!"

"The *who*?" said Elizabeth.

"It's th-this poet who keeps e-mailing us poems," explained Bennet.

"They are the absolute worst poems," said Pete. "Just listen. . . ."

Pete read the latest submission:

"Everyone shouted, 'Hey!'
Everyone, that is, but the Einsteins.
They don't know what's
going on. Al, he's thinking about the
really, really difficult science problem.
Mrs. E., she can't
believe you
said nothing about her beautiful figure
drawing. Wow, it's turned cold out.
Sunshine, you are my
sunshine. You send me lots of e-mails."

Pete peered up at Elizabeth and said, "Pretty bad, eh?"

Elizabeth was eyeing the computer screen in a peculiar manner. "I don't think this is a poem," she said.

"You're right," said Pete. "It's too awful to be a poem."

"No, I mean I think it may be a clue," she said.

Bennet glanced at Elizabeth, then focused his eyes on the computer screen. "A clue?" he said.

Elizabeth took the mouse from Pete, saying, "Look at this."

As Bennet and Pete watched, Elizabeth leaned forward and highlighted the last word in each line and put the words in bold. Here's what the message looked like after she was finished:

Everyone shouted, "**Hey!**"
Everyone, that is, but the **Einsteins.**
They don't know **what's**
going on. Al, he's thinking about **the**
really, really difficult science **problem.**
Mrs. E., she **can't**
believe **you**
said nothing about her beautiful **figure**
drawing. Wow, it's turned cold **out.**
Sunshine, you are **my**
sunshine. You send me lots of **e-mails.**

Bennet stared in amazement at the computer screen. His spine tingled.

"Yikes!" cried Pete.

Excited, Bennet grabbed the mouse out of Elizabeth's hand. "L-l-let's see what happens if we do the same thing with the Mad Poet's other messages."

He all but pushed Pete out of the chair and sat

down. He clicked on the first mysterious e-mail that they had received. He began putting the last words in each line in bold.

Is it you or is it I?
It's so hard to **think**
When you have a black **eye**
Does anyone really **know**?
The old barn owl cries who, who, **who's**
That lurking in the shadows **behind**
The red tractor? Is it **the** . . .
Nope, it's just a **pumpkin**.
Some **mystery**!

"I think I know who's behind the pumpkin mystery," Elizabeth read aloud. Then Bennet did the same with the Mad Poet's other message.

More words begin with the letter **R**
Than with the letter **U**,
But not many people are **interested**.
All they care about is getting **in**
to a school of higher **learning**.
Oh, **my**!
I just love a good **secret**!
Here's one: my faith in you is as strong as iron **ore**.
I think **not**!

"Are you interested in learning my secret or not?" said Pete.

"We've got to respond!" cried Elizabeth.

"Wait!" said Bennet. "What if it's a trick?"

"A trick?" said Elizabeth. "Why would it be a trick?"

"If this guy knows who did it, why's he telling us?" said Bennet. "I mean, doesn't *he* want to win the five-hundred-dollar prize?"

"Maybe he doesn't know about the prize," said Pete. "Or maybe it's someone who liked our Deep Doo-Doo broadcasts."

"Oh, you mean like a fan?" said Elizabeth.

"Yeah," said Pete.

"Well, maybe," said Bennet. "I guess it can't hurt to send an e-mail."

"So what should we say?" asked Elizabeth.

"Stand back!" commanded Pete, cracking his knuckles. "This is a job for Peter Eric Nickowsky."

Bennet rose, and Pete took over at the computer. He typed:

The history of
the Iroquois will be discussed during our ten course
dinner. We
hope you can
make

it. The price is five cents.
Two cents of
which will go to your
favorite charity. To reserve, send us a million e-mails.

Reading what Pete had typed, Elizabeth and Bennet laughed. Pete, pleased and smiling, continued:

So tell us what's
going on in your
life. Or is that a big
deep, dark secret?

Pete clicked on the SEND button, and the message disappeared, vanishing into cyberspace.

"Now we just have to wait and see what happens," he said.

THE WILLIAM TELL OVERTURE

That night Bennet checked his e-mail messages practically every five minutes. Each time he did, a box popped up on his computer screen with the following message: "No New Messages on Server."

At 7:35, Elizabeth called him. "Any messages?" she asked.

"Nothing," replied Bennet.

At quarter to eight, Pete called. "So did the Mad Poet e-mail us?"

"Not yet," replied Bennet.

At 8:00, Elizabeth called again.

"Still nothing," reported Bennet.

At 8:25, Pete called back.

"Still waiting," said Bennet.

At 9:00, Bennet decided that going on-line every five minutes to see if he had any e-mail messages was ridiculous. A watched computer never e-mails.

He vowed he would not go back on-line again until the next morning.

Bennet got ready for bed. He figured that after such an exciting day, he would be asleep in five minutes, tops.

Fat chance. Bennet was way too hyper to fall asleep. As he lay in the darkness, he listened to his clock radio, which was on the small table beside his bed. It was tuned to WCAC-FM, his favorite rock-and-roll radio station.

While he lay there, Bennet couldn't stop thinking about the mysterious e-mails. If the Mad Poet knew who put the pumpkin on top of the Town Hall flagpole, why didn't he or she come forward and say so? Didn't the Mad Poet want to win the $500 prize? It just didn't make any sense. Unless, of course, the Mad Poet didn't know about the prize. But if that was the case, why did the Mad Poet e-mail them in the first place?

Sometime after 10:30, the radio clicked off. Bennet was still awake—wide awake. A short time later, he heard his parents heading upstairs on their way to bed. Bennet glanced at his clock radio. The glowing green numerals said 11:05.

Bennet sighed, wishing he were asleep—or sleepy, at any rate. But he wasn't. Not even a little bit. The problem was, he couldn't get the Mad Poet off his brain. Bennet glanced at his clock radio again. It was now 11:07. Turning over in bed, he found himself staring at the dark shape that was his computer. He turned to lie on his other side. A moment later, he turned back to gaze at his computer.

Bennet couldn't stand it any longer. Forget tomorrow morning! He had to know *now* if the Mad Poet had e-mailed him.

Bennet picked up his flashlight that he kept on the table by his bed. Switching it on, he slipped out of bed and went over to his computer and sat down. He rested the flashlight on his desk so that the beam would illuminate his keyboard. He turned on his hard drive, his monitor.

The screen lit up with a sort of staticky sound. One by one, the software icons popped up in a row along the bottom of the screen. The moment his computer was ready, Bennet went on-line. He opened his e-mail.

The Mad Poet had sent another e-mail!

"Yessss!" Bennet blurted out loudly—too loudly. Fortunately, his parents hadn't heard him.

To Pete's question—"What's your big secret?"— the Mad Poet had responded:

I do not
think I run so
slow. I think I run fast.
I just love the William Tell
Overture. It makes me
want to hum. What
about you?
Let me know.

"Not so fast," Bennet whispered. "Tell me what
you know."

But what did they really know? Not much.

E-MAIL

*B*ennet didn't know what to write back. He wished Pete was there. Pete would know what to write. But Pete wasn't there, and Bennet was too excited to wait until tomorrow when Pete could write the message. Typing by flashlight, he replied:

We know the pumpkin wasn't just a prank.

He sent the message. As soon as he sent it, he realized he had forgotten to disguise his message within a poem. Bennet felt like kicking himself. How could he make such a dumb mistake? He quickly started to compose another message, this one in the form of a poem.

Bennet was racking his brain, trying to think of a line that ended with "we" when, suddenly, his computer made a soft *ping!* sound.

Bennet nearly shrieked.

The Mad Poet was on-line, right that very second!

Bennet, thrilled, clicked to see what the Mad Poet had e-mailed.

So what
do you say? Does anyone else
know how to do
the tango the way you
and I do? Please say no.

"What else do you know?" whispered Bennet.

Bennet didn't want to let on just how little they knew. He typed the following e-mail:

We know the custodian at Town Hall had
something to do with it.

Bennet had scarcely clicked the SEND button when the Mad Poet responded:

?!!???!!?

Oops, thought Bennet. Dumb guess. He quickly tried to cover up his mistake. He typed:

Just testing you.

The Mad Poet wrote back:

Hey, hey, ha, ha,
Hey, hey, ha, ha,
That's what
we say in Timbuktu. Know what else
we do?
Of course you
do. You must know.

"Ha, ha, what else do you know?" Bennet whispered. "That's the problem! Nothing!"

Desperate, frustrated, clueless, Bennet sighed. He sat back in his chair. He was wondering what he should write next when his gaze fell upon the folded newspaper that Pete had left on his desk earlier that afternoon. The paper, which was partially lit by the flashlight, was still open to the police-blotter section. In all the excitement of finding out about the Mad Poet, Bennet had completely forgotten about Mr. Abbott's stolen bicycle. He began typing.

We know about the bicycle and the records.

Bennet waited, but the Mad Poet didn't respond.

I blew it! thought Bennet. *Now the Mad Poet knows we know nothing.*

Then this message appeared on Bennet's computer screen:

Do you remember who
sang "Memories"? Was it Fred or someone else?
Stella knows,
but she won't tell me. Maybe one day I
will remember. By the way, I took
photos of a cat the other day. Want to see them?

Bennet stared at his computer screen. He was shocked. He mouthed the words: "Who else knows I took them?"

The Mad Poet was the thief!

LET'S MAKE A DEAL

Recovering from his surprise, Bennet swiftly sent off another e-mail.

No one. Just us.

A moment later, he got this e-mail:

Do you live in the U.S.?

Bennet was puzzled. What on earth did the United States have to do with anything? Then he realized that the Mad Poet wasn't referring to the United States of America. He meant *us!*

Bennet typed:

Just my friends and me.

The Mad Poet responded:

Hey, let's
you and I make
a sand castle. I know of a
great beach where you don't have to deal
with flies. Who shall
we ask to join us? I'd like to ask Orville. Can we?

"Let's make a deal, shall we?" Bennet read
aloud. He quickly typed:

What kind of a deal?

Here's what the Mad Poet e-mailed back:

Do be do be do
I love to sing and you?
Do you still
love to have
people over to that
crazy tree house of yours? Does Count Dracula
still wear that silly Frankenstein mask?
Do you know where he got it from?
I think he got it at the
shopping mall—that one deep
in the heart of Texas. Do
be do be do . . .
I should sing on Saturday opera broadcasts.

"Do you still have the Dracula mask from the Deep Doo-Doo broadcasts?" whispered Bennet.

"Yes," he wrote back.

The Mad Poet replied:

Some will,
some won't. Me? I'm happy to trade
you my
favorite Ken Griffey, Jr. baseball card for your secret
cotton-candy recipe. Is it three or four
cups of sugar? Speaking of secrets, is that your
real face or is it a mask?
Now shuffle the cards and deal!

"Will trade my secret for your mask," whispered Bennet. "Deal?"

"Deal!" he typed back.

It took forever for the Mad Poet to answer—so long, in fact, that Bennet wondered if the Mad Poet had gone off-line. But he hadn't. It had just taken him a while to write his next message. Here's what it said:

The look
that's in
your eyes is the
same look you had in the bushes

that day we hid by
the swing set and scared the
daylights out of those school
kids who were playing basketball
on the old asphalt court.
Hey, think it'll snow tomorrow?
If it does, I hope it starts after
I get home at 5:00.

"Look in the bushes by the school basketball court tomorrow after five," whispered Bennet.

"What will we find?" Bennet wrote back.

The Mad Poet responded:

I hope you'll
come visit me by the sea.
And don't
you dare forget
to bring the
suntan lotion and my scuba mask.

EUREKA!

The next day at five minutes past 5:00, Bennet and Pete returned to school on their bikes. They took Gus with them. Two hours earlier, the school had been humming with activity. But now there wasn't a kid or teacher around.

The sun had set, but there was still plenty of light in the sky. A band of rosy clouds stretched across the sky above the far end of the soccer field.

"I still don't understand why the Mad Poet wants your Dracula mask," said Pete as they pedaled up to the school.

"I don't understand it, either," replied Bennet. "But that's what he asked for."

Elizabeth was supposed to meet them at the bike racks by the main entrance. But she wasn't there. Nor was her bike.

"Where is she?" asked Bennet as he hopped off his bike. "I told her to be here at five."

"I'm right here," Elizabeth's voice replied. She

stepped out from behind a maple tree that was by the bike racks.

Bennet nearly jumped out of his skin.

"Wh-wh-what are you trying to do?" he cried. "Scare us half to death?"

"Sorry. I didn't realize you were so jumpy."

"I'm not j-j-jumpy!" protested Bennet. "I'm just—just being careful!"

"You seem jumpy."

"Well, I'm not!"

"Okay, if you say so," replied Elizabeth.

They walked behind the gymnasium to the outdoor basketball court.

"So where did the Mad Poet say to look?" asked Elizabeth.

"Shh, not so loud," said Bennet. "We don't want the whole world to hear."

"Where did the Mad Poet say to look?" Elizabeth asked again, whispering this time.

"In the bushes by the basketball court," replied Bennet.

"Well, here's the basketball court," said Elizabeth as she stepped onto the blacktop court.

"And here are the bushes," said Pete. He walked over to some bushes at the edge of the woods. The bushes were a bright, fiery red.

Pete and Elizabeth began searching in the

bushes. Bennet, meanwhile, shuffled his feet in the leaves that were on the ground.

If only the Mad Poet could've been a little more specific, he was wishing to himself when, suddenly, he heard a kid's voice. He stopped shuffling and listened. Now he heard another voice.

"Someone's coming!" he said in alarm.

Two boys on bikes came flying around the corner of the brick school. A collie trotted behind, racing to keep up.

"P-p-pretend we're looking for a ball," whispered Bennet.

"Where is that darn ball?" cried Pete.

The boys pedaled past, with the collie right behind them. Gus, barking, bounded after the collie.

"Gus, come back here!" yelled Pete.

Pete started after Gus. He was dashing out of the bushes when he stumbled. He fell, face first, onto the ground. Fortunately, he landed on the grass.

Bennet and Elizabeth raced over to him. "You okay?" asked Elizabeth.

"Yeah, I'm fine," replied Pete, getting to his feet. He was more embarrassed than hurt.

By now, the two boys and the collie were halfway across the baseball field. They were heading for an opening in the chain-link fence that bordered the edge of left field. Gus, panting, his tongue hanging out, walked back to Pete. Pete shook his finger and said, "Bad dog!"

Gus just wagged his tail.

"Man, what did I trip on, anyway?" asked Pete as he poked about in the bushes.

"Hey!" he cried out, bending down. He stood up with a big brown envelope in his hand. He waved the envelope excitedly in the air. "Eureka! Look what I found!"

"This must be what we're looking for!" said Elizabeth.

Pete squished the envelope with his fingers. "Feels like a book," he said.

Pete would have opened the envelope right then and there had it not been for Bennet.

"Not here!" he cried, glancing about nervously. He had the uneasy feeling that they were being watched. "W-w-we'll open it back at my house."

Bennet unzipped his backpack, removed the Dracula mask that was inside, and set it in the bushes.

DRUMROLL, PLEASE!

If Bennet and Pete had been alone, they would have been back at Bennet's house in less than five minutes. But because they were with Elizabeth—who didn't have her bike—they had to walk.

"I don't know why you didn't b-bring your bike," said Bennet.

"Nobody told me to," replied Elizabeth as they walked past a parked car. The back bumper had a sticker that said: SET A GOOD EXAMPLE: VOTE AB-BOTT.

It was dark by the time they reached Bennet's house. The garage door was open, and the light in the garage was on. His mother's minivan was parked in the garage. The other half of the garage was empty. Mr. Ordway wasn't home from work yet.

The newspaper carrier had left the Ordways' paper on their driveway. Bennet picked it up as he wheeled his bike into the garage. He put his bike away by the lawn mower and then unfolded the paper.

For the past few days, the front page of *The Sun* had been running a special section that featured theories on who might have put the pumpkin on top of the Town Hall flagpole. The theories had been submitted by readers. Most of them were jokes. Today's theory was that space aliens had flown down in a UFO to get some Halloween pumpkins to take back to their home planet. One of the pumpkins had accidentally dropped from the spaceship. On its fall to earth, the pumpkin had been speared by the flagpole.

Bennet glanced at his watch. It was nearly 6:00. He knew his mother was probably in the kitchen getting dinner ready. So instead of going into the house through the garage, which would have brought them into the kitchen, Bennet, Pete, and Elizabeth quietly entered through the front door. Bennet knew what would happen if his mother saw Elizabeth again. She would start asking all the questions she hadn't gotten to ask the day before. Elizabeth would never get past the kitchen.

While Pete and Elizabeth slipped upstairs, Bennet popped his head into the kitchen. His mother was at the counter, chopping up some carrots.

While she cooked, she was watching the little television set that was by the kitchen table.

"Hey, Mom, I'm home," said Bennet.

Before his mother had a chance to engage him in a lengthy conversation about how school was and did he have any homework, Bennet was gone.

Up in Bennet's bedroom, Pete and Elizabeth were sitting on the floor, waiting for Bennet. The envelope was sitting on Pete's lap. Bennet shut the door behind him, walked over to the window, and drew the curtains. Then he sat down on the floor beside Pete and Elizabeth.

"Well," said Pete as he picked up the envelope, "let's see what we have here, shall we? Drumroll, please."

"J-j-just open it, will you," said Bennet impatiently.

"And the envelope contains . . ."

"A college yearbook?" said Elizabeth as Pete pulled out a book. The front cover had a photograph of a leafy college campus. HAVERMEYER COLLEGE 1974, it said in big letters.

A yellow Post-it note was sticking out from one of the pages. Pete opened to that page and found several folded sheets of notebook paper. He unfolded them.

It was another poem. A very long poem.

OH, MY GOODNESS!

Pete stood up, cleared his voice, and began to read the poem aloud. He spoke in a deep, theatrical voice. It was the sort of voice a hammy actor might use—or a boy trying to make a pretty girl smile.

"Greetings, one and all!
It is so good of you
to have
me here. Unfortunately, my two
pet boas had things to do
and couldn't make it. Is
that not rude? Sometimes I'd like to put
those two knuckleheads in the
zoo. I'm wearing polka dots
today—just for you. We should get together
more often and
talk about important stuff like . . . figure
skating. I really need to get out

to the

rink and do a few double lutzes. It's a mystery

why I never do. But I

am sure you have found

that this

is true for you, too. Hey, I thought of a wonderful

idea. I'm going to write a book!

Don't worry, you'll be in

it along with

your good friend Dracula, who still has some

of my favorite old record LPs.

Did you hear that

just recently

I came

home and went into

the living room and found my

two pet boas dancing to my favorite possession?

Yes, my Britney Spears CD! I

couldn't believe it! You can't,

either? Whatever you do, don't expose

yourself to ultraviolet rays the way I myself

have done. You didn't just say, "Yuck!"

did you? I thought I heard a "Yuck!"

Say, why is it when you and

I play chess I never win?

Is it because I refuse to move the

pawns? What if I paid you $500?

Would you let me win the grand prize
and checkmate you? You say yes but
I know better. Here's something <u>you</u>
don't know. I can
beat you at checkers. Consider yourself lucky
I have never played you!"

Pete came to the end of the poem and looked up. "Another Mad Poet masterpiece!" he said.

Elizabeth wasted no time deciphering the poem. "All you have to do is put the dots together and figure out the mystery," she said. "I found this wonderful book in with some LPs that recently came into my possession. I can't expose myself—yuck! yuck!—and win the five-hundred-dollar prize, but *you* can. Lucky you!"

"Why can't he reveal himself and win the five-hundred-dollar prize?" asked Pete.

"Because if he does, he'll probably be arrested," said Bennet.

"Why?" said Pete.

"For st-stealing Mr. Abbott's bike and old records," said Bennet. "The only reason he knows what he knows is because he broke into Mr. Abbott's garage."

"So all *we* have to do is figure out what *he* knows," said Pete.

"He said all we have to do is connect the dots," said Elizabeth.

"Yeah, but what dots?" said Pete.

"Maybe there's something on the page he stickered," suggested Bennet.

The page contained row after row of small, black-and-white rectangular photographs. Each photo was a head shot of a student. Most of the students were looking straight into the camera, smiling.

"I don't see anything unusual," Pete started to say when he abruptly cried out: "Wait a sec! Look who I see!"

He tapped his finger on one of the photographs in the second row.

"It's Mr. Abbott!" said Elizabeth.

It was indeed Mr. Abbott. He looked much younger. Not only that, but he had a mustache and dark hair that was practically touching his shoulders.

"Wow, look how young he looks!" said Elizabeth.

"L-l-look how long his hair is!" said Bennet.

Pete read aloud the caption under the photo.

" 'Robert J. Abbott. Bobby. Most Likely to Succeed. President of the Rock Climbing Club. "Go for it!" Pink Floyd rules!' "

"That's not much of a clue," said Elizabeth.

"No," agreed Bennet.

"There's got to be something else in this year-book," said Pete.

He began flipping pages.

"Oh, my goodness!" he suddenly blurted out, his eyes bulging.

In just seconds, Pete's face had turned as red as the bushes in which they had discovered the year-book.

What is it?" asked Elizabeth as, leaning over, she peered at the page.

Her eyes widened. She looked shocked.

"Oh, *my!*" she gasped, placing her hand over her mouth.

"Show me! Show me!" cried Bennet.

Pete turned the yearbook around so Bennet could see.

Bennet's mouth dropped open.

It was a photograph of Mr. Abbott. Like the other photograph, this one showed him with long hair and a mustache. In this picture, though, he was wearing a zany *Cat in the Hat* top hat.

But it wasn't what he was wearing that was so shocking. It was what he *wasn't* wearing. He was not wearing anything at all! He was stark naked! The photograph had captured Mr. Abbott sprinting across a classroom in front of a very startled-looking professor. The caption read: "Streaking 101—As anyone who's ever taken a class with Professor Charles Walrath knows, it isn't easy to surprise the history professor. But here's one student who found a way."

"Wh-what's he doing without any clothes on?" asked Bennet, aghast.

"He must be streaking!" said Pete gleefully.

"*Streaking?*" said Elizabeth. "What's streaking?"

"You've never heard of streaking?" said Pete.

"What is it?" asked Bennet.

"That's what people our parents' age used to do in college," said Pete.

"M-my parents never did this!" said Bennet.

"Have you asked them?"

"Well, no," said Bennet. "But I know they never have."

"Mine, neither," said Elizabeth.

"Well, you never know," said Pete. "Many people our parents' age did streak. It was a big college fad back in the 1970s."

"How do you know so much about this?" asked Elizabeth.

"Haven't you ever seen that old photograph that was taken at the Academy Awards?"

Bennet and Elizabeth both shook their heads.

"It's so famous," said Pete. "I can't believe you guys haven't seen it. It shows this guy without any clothes running across the stage. That's how I found out about it. I saw the photograph, and I asked my mom."

"Someone really ran naked in front of the TV cameras?" said Elizabeth.

"Wow," said Bennet.

Pete laughed at their reaction. "I'm telling you it was a big fad," he said. "Hey, you would've done it, too, if you were in college back then."

"I would not!" replied Elizabeth.

"I—I—I can't believe Mr. Abbott would have done such a thing," said Bennet. "I mean, y-y-you heard him at the debate. He's the candidate who says he's going to set a good example for today's youth."

"Which is exactly why he doesn't want anyone to find out about this picture," said Pete.

"At least not right before the election," said Elizabeth.

"I guess it would be kind of embarrassing for him," said Bennet.

"Kind of?" said Pete. "Try *extremely* embarrassing."

"I bet you anything that's why he didn't mention anything about his bike being stolen," said Pete. "Hey, if someone had a picture of me naked, I'd keep my mouth shut, too."

"Yeah, but if that's the case," said Bennet, "wh-why did he report the robbery in the first place?"

Elizabeth responded: "He probably didn't realize the yearbook was stolen until after he reported the robbery to the police."

"Say, you don't think . . ." Pete started to say, but then he shook his head and said, "Nah. It's too crazy."

"What is?" asked Bennet.

"It's not even worth bringing up," said Pete.

"Let's hear it," said Elizabeth.

"Well . . . okay," said Pete. "I was just wondering . . . well, what if Mr. Abbott is our pumpkin man?"

"*Mr. Abbott?*" exclaimed Elizabeth.

"No way!" said Bennet.

"No, listen," said Pete. "We're looking for a diversion, right?"

"Yeah?" said Elizabeth.

"Well, maybe Mr. Abbott put the pumpkin on top of the flagpole to create a diversion in case his stolen yearbook ever did become public," said Pete.

"Not Mr. Abbott!" said Bennet. "He would never climb up a flagpole!"

"I don't know," said Elizabeth. "I think Pete may be onto something. What if Mr. Abbott felt he had no choice? What if he wanted to make sure the press had a juicy story so they wouldn't pay attention if his college yearbook popped up? Can you imagine what would happen if the press found out about this? They'd have a field day!"

"I can see the headlines now," cried Pete. " 'Abbott on a Streak!' 'Abbott Bares All!' 'The Naked Truth About Abbott!' "

They all broke up with laughter.

"Well, wh-when you put it that way," said Bennet, "maybe Mr. Abbott *is* our pumpkin man."

"Yeah," said Elizabeth excitedly. "And don't forget—he was the president of his college's rock-climbing club!"

"That's right!" said Pete. "A flagpole would be a piece of cake for him to shimmy up."

"But why didn't the Mad Poet send the yearbook to the newspapers?" asked Elizabeth.

"B-b-because he wanted to trade it for my Dracula mask," said Bennet.

"So here's what must've happened," said Pete, trying to connect the dots. "The Mad Poet broke into Mr. Abbott's garage and stole his bike and record albums."

Elizabeth picked up the story. "When the Mad Poet got home, he found Mr. Abbott's old college yearbook mixed in with the record albums."

At this point, Bennet took over. "H-he started flipping through the yearbook and found the picture of Mr. Abbott streaking."

Now Pete jumped in: "Meanwhile, Mr. Abbott reported the robbery to the police. But then he discovered his college yearbook was also missing."

Elizabeth cut in: "He knew how ridiculous he'd look if the yearbook surfaced before the election."

"So," said Bennet, taking over, "to d-d-divert everyone's attention, he created a cover-up: he put the pumpkin up on top of the flagpole."

"Which he had no trouble doing, since he used to be a rock climber," said Pete.

"The Mad Poet knows Mr. Abbott put the p-p-pumpkin up on the flagpole," said Bennet.

"But he can't come forward and say who did it and get the five-hundred-dollar prize," said Elizabeth. "Because if he did—"

"H-he'd get arrested!" Bennet blurted out.

"But while *he* can't come forward—*we* can!" cried Pete, grinning like a maniac.

"And win the five-hundred-dollar prize!" said Elizabeth.

"I'll put it on the Deep Doo-Doo Web site," said Pete.

"I'll put out a special edition of *The Purple Patch*," said Elizabeth.

"Aren't you two f-f-forgetting something?" asked Bennet.

"That's right—the Dracula mask!" said Pete. "We still don't know why the Mad Poet wanted it."

"That's not what I was getting at," said Bennet. "If we report this, everyone will want to know how *we* found out about it."

"Yeah, so?" said Pete. "We'll just say we found a yearbook in some bushes."

"A yearbook that was stolen out of a garage," Bennet reminded him.

"You think people will think *we* stole it?" asked Elizabeth.

"Wouldn't you think that?" asked Bennet.

"Oh, my gosh!" said Pete. "There's no way we can report this story!"

"Or collect the five-hundred-dollar prize," said Bennet.

"Unless . . ." said Elizabeth.

Her face lit up as if she had just had the most brilliant idea.

THE PHONE CALL

"ere, give me the yearbook," said Elizabeth.

Pete handed it to her. She began flipping the pages. Then, turning to Bennet, she said: "Can I use your phone?"

"Sure," said Bennet. He opened the bottom drawer of his desk and took out an old pink Princess telephone. He unhooked the telephone line from his modem and plugged it into the phone. He listened to make sure it had a dial tone. It did. He handed the phone to Elizabeth.

She pushed back her blond hair, placed the receiver to her ear, and dialed 411.

"Hello," she said, "could I have the area code for New Hampshire?"

"New Hampshire!" cried Pete. "Who the heck are you calling?"

Elizabeth didn't respond. She sat down at Bennet's desk and picked up a pencil. She jotted down "603" on a piece of paper. Then she pressed the dial-tone button on the receiver and dialed 603-555-1212.

"Cornish Falls," she said into the phone. "Hello, could I have the phone number of a Mr. Charles Walrath?" She listened for a moment, then wrote down a number. "Thank you," she said to the operator, and hung up.

She began dialing again.

"Wh-what are you doing?" asked Bennet.

"I'm calling Mr. Charles Walrath," said Elizabeth.

She held up the yearbook. It was open to Mr. Abbott's streaking photograph. She pointed to the shocked-looking professor who was also in the photograph. "According to this caption, *this* is Mr. Charles Walrath. I figured that, being a college professor, he might still live near the college. And he does."

"Y-y-you're really going to call him?" asked Bennet.

"Sure, why not?" said Elizabeth. "I'll just say I'm writing this article about one of his old students."

"I get it!" said Pete. "That way *he* can tell you about how Mr. Abbott streaked in his class. I'm sure he hasn't forgotten *that*."

"You got it!" said Elizabeth, smiling. "No one will ever know we saw the yearbook."

"Elizabeth, you're a genius!" gushed Pete.

Those weren't exactly the words Bennet would have chosen. Still, much as he hated to admit it, it was a pretty clever idea.

Elizabeth was about to dial the number when Pete reached over and pressed the dial-tone button.

"Allow me," he said in a very gentlemanly manner. He held out his hand for the receiver.

Elizabeth handed him the phone.

Pete dialed the number. "It's ringing," he reported. "Someone's picking up!"

Pete began speaking into the phone. But he didn't speak in his normal voice. He lowered it to sound much older. He sounded like a middle-aged man—with a bit of an British accent.

"Hello, may I speak with Charlie, please?" he said.

"Wh-wh-what are you doing?" whispered Bennet in alarm. He tried to grab the phone from Pete.

Pete just smiled and waved Bennet away like he was an annoying housefly. He was showing off in front of Elizabeth.

Pete went on:

"Yes, is Charlie there? Charlie Walrath? Oh, dear, I meant to say Chuck."

It was all Pete could do to keep from breaking out into uncontrollable giggles. He put his palm over the mouthpiece of the phone and whispered in his normal voice: "I got his wife."

"Who am I?" said Pete, disguising his voice again as he spoke into the phone. "I'm an old college student of the professor's. I was hoping we could catch up on old times. Is he there, by any chance?"

Pete, listening, said, "Oh!" Then, still listening, he added: "Oh, dear!" and "I had no idea!"

"Well, I'm terribly sorry to hear this," said Pete. "Please give him my best the next time you see him. Thank you."

And with that, he hung up.

"What happened?" asked Elizabeth.

"Wh-what did she say?" demanded Bennet.

"He's in a nursing home," said Pete.

"Poor guy," said Elizabeth.

"His wife said that, even if I could talk to him, he doesn't remember much anymore. She got very sad," said Pete.

"It *is* sad," said Elizabeth. "My grandmother has trouble remembering stuff, too."

"Well, so much for that idea," said Bennet.

"No, not necessarily," said Elizabeth.

Pete grinned mischievously. "You're not thinking what I think you're thinking, are you?" he said.

"I don't know," replied Elizabeth. "What do you think I'm thinking?"

"I think you're thinking of calling the nursing home. Am I right?"

Elizabeth shook her head and said, "No."

Pete looked disappointed.

"What *are* you thinking?" asked Bennet.

"I'm thinking *we* know that Mr. Abbott's old college professor is in a nursing home, but I'll bet you anything Mr. Abbott doesn't know it."

"What are you saying?" said Bennet.

"I'm saying we can bluff it," said Elizabeth.

"Hey, I like this idea!" said Pete.

"Well, I don't," said Bennet. "I-i-it sounds dangerous! Besides, I don't care what Abbott did in college. I just want to link him to the pumpkin. And w-we still can't do that."

"Maybe we can't," said Pete. "But I know someone who can."

"Who?" asked Elizabeth.

"Mr. Abbott himself," said Pete, with a devilish gleam in his eye.

And then he explained how.

A STARTLING DISCOVERY

Since it was a Friday, Bennet got to stay up later than usual that night. So as not to arouse his mother and father's suspicions, he spent the early part of the evening in the living room watching TV. That's how, if he wasn't doing anything with Pete, he normally would have spent a Friday evening.

The rest of the evening, however, Bennet spent up in his bedroom, with the door locked and his radio on. He sat on the floor with his newest invention—a battery-operated fan that had Kleenexes wrapped around its blades. Bennet called it the "Fingerprint Eraser." He had invented it just that evening. He was using it to clean Mr. Abbott's old college yearbook of fingerprint smudges. He didn't want anyone tracing the yearbook back to him, Pete, or Elizabeth. To make sure he didn't leave any fingerprints while using the Fingerprint Eraser, Bennet wore his winter gloves.

It was nearly midnight by the time he finished. In all probability, Bennet would have finished much sooner if he had simply wiped the pages off by hand. But that was an inventor for you—he had to do it his own innovative way.

Bennet slipped the yearbook into the brown envelope that they had found it in. Then he wiped off the envelope. He unzipped his backpack and removed his digital camera and everything else that was inside it, then stuck in the envelope.

. . .

Bennet had intended to wake up super early the next morning. But he was so tired from staying up late the night before that he slept right through the alarm on his clock radio. He didn't wake up until almost 10:00. He probably would have slept even later if his mother hadn't tapped on his door and said, "Bennet, you awake?"

"Mnn," he replied groggily, and pulled up his bedcovers.

"You have a phone call. It's Elizabeth."

That sure woke Bennet up fast! He hopped out of bed and hurried into his parents' bedroom and picked up the phone.

"We're on," said Elizabeth.

"We're on?"

"I finally got through to Mr. Abbott. He's agreed to meet with us. But he can only do it this morning at his house. We have to go now."

"I'll call Pete," said Bennet.

"I already have," replied Elizabeth. "His sister, Emma, is driving us over there."

"How come you w-w-waited so long to call me?" asked Bennet.

"I called you earlier, but your mom said you were sleeping. I told her not to wake you. I know how you need your beauty rest."

"Funny," said Bennet.

"Anyway," said Elizabeth, "we're all waiting for you outside your house."

Bennet stepped over to the window. Elizabeth was on his front lawn, holding a cell phone to her ear. Pete was standing beside her. Emma was at the wheel of the Nickowskys' station wagon, which was parked in front of his house. Pete grinned and waved.

"I'll be right down," said Bennet.

"Don't forget the you-know-what," said Elizabeth.

On the way over to Mr. Abbott's house, Bennet, Pete, and Elizabeth sat in the backseat and went over the plan that they had devised the day before. The plan called for Bennet and Elizabeth to talk to Mr. Abbott and try to get him to confess about the pumpkin. Pete, meanwhile, was to sneak into the Abbotts' garage and return the yearbook.

Rather than ditching the yearbook in some Dumpster or burying it, they had decided to return it to Mr. Abbott. After all, it was *his* yearbook. Bennet, Pete, and Elizabeth were not interested in making the yearbook public and embarrassing Mr. Abbott. They simply wanted a confession about the pumpkin.

Bennet gave Pete his backpack. "You got the c-c-camcorder?" he asked.

"Right here," said Pete, taking it out of his backpack.

The plan was for Bennet to film Mr. Abbott while Elizabeth interviewed him.

Bennet checked to make sure the camcorder was working. He couldn't get it to turn on. "Hey, the battery's dead!" he cried.

"It is?" said Pete, surprised.

"Didn't you check it?" asked Bennet.

"I guess I forgot," replied Pete.

Bennet let out an exasperated *ugh!* "I can't believe you f-f-forgot to recharge the battery!"

"So sue me," said Pete, who, like Bennet, was very nervous.

Bennet couldn't even use his digital camera—he had left it at home.

"It's okay," said Elizabeth. "We'll interview him without a camera."

Elizabeth had written down the directions to Mr. Abbott's house on a piece of yellow lined paper. The Abbotts lived on a quiet, dead-end street on the other side of the Agaming River, which flowed through town. Their house, number 25, was a brown, shingled saltbox with pine trees growing all about. It was at the end of the street, near the turn-around.

"Keep the motor running," Pete instructed Emma as he, Bennet, and Elizabeth hopped out of the car. "Just in case."

"Just in case of *what?*" asked Emma. They had not told her what they were up to. All she knew was that they were here to interview Mr. Abbott the mayoral candidate.

Pete slung Bennet's backpack around his shoulder. "Good luck!" he said to Bennet and Elizabeth.

"Good luck to you, too!" said Elizabeth.

"Yeah, good luck!" said Bennet.

They went their separate ways—Pete headed down the street with Mr. Abbott's yearbook inside Bennet's backpack; Bennet and Elizabeth walked across Mr. Abbott's lawn to his front door.

"Better let me do all the talking," said Elizabeth.

"Wh-what?" said Bennet. "You scared I'm going to blow it?"

"I didn't say that," replied Elizabeth.

"Yeah, but th-that's what you think."

Elizabeth rang the doorbell. "It is not," she said.

"It is so."

"It is not."

"It is—" Bennet started to say when, suddenly, the front door opened, and there stood Mr. Abbott.

FAST THINKING

Mr. Abbott looked as if he had just come in from jogging: he was dressed in red jogging shorts, a navy-blue nylon jacket, running shoes, and a baseball cap. He was much bigger than Bennet remembered. He was also very muscular. He looked like he would have no trouble climbing up a flagpole.

"Hi, Mr. Abbott, it's me: Elizabeth Smith."

Mr. Abbott smiled and shook her hand. "Glad to see you again, Elizabeth," he said.

Bennet stepped forward, holding out his hand. "And I'm Bennet Ordway. W-we met at the debate."

"Oh, sure," said Mr. Abbott, giving Bennet a hearty handshake. "Come on in, guys," he said, holding the door open for them. "My wife's taken the kids to their soccer practice."

Mr. Abbott led the way into a large living room. "Can I get you something to drink?" he asked.

"No, thanks," replied Bennet.

"We have some bagels left over from breakfast. Want some?"

"No, thank you," said Elizabeth.

"We're talking cinnamon raisin here," said Mr. Abbott. "You sure you don't want any?"

Bennet smiled. Mr. Abbott seemed like a nice guy. Both he and Elizabeth said they were sure they didn't want a bagel.

"Okay, then, let's talk," said Mr. Abbott.

Bennet and Elizabeth sat down on the living-room couch. It was a big, comfy couch, with a cheerful flowery design. At one end of the couch stood a table that was covered with framed photographs of Mr. Abbott and his family. One photograph showed them standing on top of a mountain, facing the camera and smiling, with an awesome mountain range in the distance. There was another photograph of Mr. Abbott, alone, rappelling down what appeared to be a dangerously steep cliff.

Mr. Abbott sat down in an armchair by the brick fireplace. Bennet noticed that a Band-Aid on Mr. Abbott's left shin was beginning to peel off. He wondered if he should tell Mr. Abbott about it.

Mr. Abbott crossed his legs and, smiling, said, "So what did you want to ask me?"

Just then, outside the house, loud barking erupted. It sounded vicious as anything.

"You have a dog?" said Bennet.

"Yeah, a Doberman," replied Mr. Abbott. "I keep him in the garage."

Elizabeth glanced at Bennet. "The garage?"

"I got him right after—well, no need to go into that. He's a good dog, but he barks incessantly. So, anyway, what did you want to ask me?"

"Well," said Elizabeth. She looked very nervous all of a sudden. She was worried about Pete, Bennet could tell. "As I—um—said over the—um—phone, we're about to . . . ah . . . um . . . um . . ."

"P-p-print a story," said Bennet.

"Yes, that's right, print a story," said Elizabeth. "And—um—we'd like to get your comment on it."

Mr. Abbott seemed distracted by the barking. He got up from his chair.

"Excuse me," he said. "I just want to see what that darn dog is barking at."

Bennet knew what the dog was barking at—Pete. He also knew that, to protect Pete, he had to do something, and fast.

But what?

Mr. Abbott was about to leave the living room when Bennet blurted out:

"Did y-y-you get the dog because of your robbery?"

Mr. Abbott froze in his tracks. He swung around, with a startled look on his face. He stared at Bennet with the most penetrating eyes. It was really scary.

"How did you know my house was broken into?" he asked.

NO COMMENT

I-i-it was in the police blotter," replied Bennet quickly. "Y-y-you know, in the n-newspaper."

"It said you had a bicycle stolen," added Elizabeth.

"A brand-new bike, too," grumbled Mr. Abbott.

"Was anything else taken?" asked Elizabeth.

Mr. Abbott regarded her suspiciously. "Yes. Some of my old record albums."

"Anything else?" asked Elizabeth.

"Why do you ask?"

"Just asking," replied Elizabeth. "Remember, I'm a reporter for my school newspaper. It's my job to ask questions."

By now, the dog was really barking up a storm. "I'll be right back," said Mr. Abbott, and left the room.

Elizabeth turned to Bennet. She looked scared.

"Poor Pete," she said.

"He'll be okay," said Bennet.

Bennet had been worried about Pete, too, but he wasn't anymore. That's because he had remembered something about his friend. Pete was a *dog person.* If anyone knew how to tame a vicious Doberman pinscher, it was Pete. Pete *loved* dogs.

From another part of the house, they heard Mr. Abbott shout: "King! Stop it now!"

A moment later, Mr. Abbott returned, saying, "Must've been a chipmunk."

Yeah, a chipmunk named Pete, thought Bennet.

"So what's this story you're planning to write?" asked Mr. Abbott, taking his seat. "I hope it's not about my garage being robbed."

"No," said Elizabeth. "We think we've solved the mystery of who stuck the pumpkin on top of the Town Hall flagpole."

"Oh, really?" said Mr. Abbott, eyeing them with interest. "Good for you. Whom do you suspect?"

"You!" blurted out Bennet, without thinking.

Bennet knew he had made a terrible mistake the moment he had spoken. He also knew that this was not how Elizabeth had planned to get Mr. Abbott to make his pumpkin confession. He could almost hear Elizabeth groaning to herself.

If Mr. Abbott was taken aback by Bennet's accusation, he didn't let on. He didn't even bat an eye. He just laughed. Could it be that they were wrong about him?

"That's ridiculous," he said. "Why on earth would I do a thing like that?"

"We think you did it to hide something," said Elizabeth.

"Hide what?" asked Mr. Abbott.

"We're hoping you might be able to tell us that," said Elizabeth.

"Well, I hate to disappoint you," said Mr. Abbott, "but there's nothing to tell." He lifted the cuff of his running jacket and examined his wristwatch. "I'm afraid that's all the time I can give you," he said, getting up.

The interview over, Mr. Abbott walked Bennet and Elizabeth to the front door. Out on the street, Pete was leaning against the side of the car, waiting. When he saw Bennet and Elizabeth step out of the house, he hopped into the backseat.

"Well, kids, sorry you had to come all this way for such a short interview," said Mr. Abbott.

"Could I ask you one more question?" asked Elizabeth.

"I really need to get going," replied Mr. Abbott.

"It'll only take a second," said Elizabeth. "After I interviewed you the other day, I decided to do a more in-depth article on you. You know, like a profile."

"Why?"

"I told you: I'm a reporter," she said. "So I called your old college. I was shocked what I found out. Particularly what you did in front of your old college professor—a Mr. Charles Walrath."

Mr. Abbott's eyes widened. "You *called* my old college professor? What do you know?"

"Oh, I think *you* know," replied Elizabeth. She flipped open her little notepad. "Care to comment?" she asked, peering up, her pen poised.

"No, I would not!" replied Mr. Abbott crossly.

"No . . . I . . . would . . . not," repeated Elizabeth, writing it down, word for word, in her notepad. She even included an exclamation point. She shut the notepad and looked up. "Okay, thanks," she said, smiling. With that, she swung around and began to make a beeline across the front lawn for the Nickowskys' car.

Bennet found himself standing alone with Mr. Abbott. Once again, he noticed the peeling Band-Aid on the man's shin.

Bennet pointed to it and said, "Y-you know, Mr. Abbott, you might want to change that Band-Aid streak. D-d-did I say *streak*? I meant Band-Aid strip! *Strip*? N-no, no, not *strip*! I meant—*never mind!* Well, th-thanks f-f-for talking with us." Bennet quickly hurried off after Elizabeth.

He heard the front door slam. It scared the daylights out of Bennet. It also scared Elizabeth. The two of them broke into a dash for the car.

"What happened? What did he say?" Pete asked as he slid over to make room for Elizabeth and Bennet in the backseat.

"Quick, get out of here!" cried Bennet, shutting the door behind him.

Emma, however, was not one for making a fast getaway. First, she insisted that they all buckle up. Then she turned her head to make sure no cars were coming. This on a quiet, dead-end street. Putting on her blinker, Emma cautiously, slowly, pulled out. She drove to the end of the street and made a flawless three-point turn at the turnaround. As they drove back, Bennet was too frightened to peek over at Mr. Abbott's house.

"Will one of you please tell me what happened?" demanded Pete.

"H-h-he got m-m-mad at us, okay?" said Bennet.

"He did? Really?" said Pete. "And to think he told everyone at the debate he wasn't a hothead."

"What do you mean he got mad at you?" asked Emma, glancing back at them.

"H-h-he got mad at us," said Bennet.

"Did he confess about the pumpkin?" asked Pete.

"No, he didn't," said Elizabeth.

"You mean, we still can't connect him to the pumpkin?" said Pete.

"No," replied Elizabeth. She glared at Bennet to let him know whose fault *that* was.

They had left Mr. Abbott's street. Now they were driving through a heavily wooded area, along a winding, unpopulated road. The foliage was breathtaking—yellows, reds, oranges, golds, and salmons —that's assuming, of course, a person was interested in the autumn colors.

"What's your problem, you jerk?" Emma suddenly said, addressing her rearview mirror.

Bennet turned his head. A big, dark green Jeep Grand Cherokee was tailgating them. Bennet nearly had a heart attack when he saw who was at the wheel. Mr. Abbott!

He looked furious.

A BLUFF ON A BLUFF

Speed up!" yelled Bennet.

"I am not speeding up!" Emma yelled right back. "I'm pulling over and letting this creep pass."

Bennet, Pete, and Elizabeth all shouted *"No!"* at the top of their lungs.

"Whatever you do, *don't* stop!" said Bennet.

"Why, what is going on?" demanded Emma.

"That's Abbott!" cried Bennet.

"He's angry at us," said Elizabeth. "He thinks we're going to write a bad story about him."

"Nobody told me this," said Emma. "You should've told me this. I never would have agreed to drive here if—hey, pal, back off!" she blurted out, gazing into her rearview mirror.

Bennet, Elizabeth, and Pete all swung around. Mr. Abbott had sped up.

"Oh, no, *he's* no hothead!" cried Pete.

Emma was close to tears. "They never told me how to handle something like *this* in driver's ed!"

"Wait a sec!" said Bennet. "What are we so w-w-worried about? Abbott has nothing on us. Pete returned the yearbook."

"Uh, actually, Alva, I didn't," said Pete.

Bennet stared at him. "Wh-what do you mean you didn't?"

"I didn't return it," said Pete. "I couldn't get into the garage. There was this dog. I couldn't get past him."

"Wh-wh-what do you mean you couldn't get past him?" said Bennet. "Y-y-you're a *dog person*! You *love* dogs!"

"I love black Labs, yes," agreed Pete. "Doberman pinschers, no."

Elizabeth cut in. "So you mean you still have Mr. Abbott's yearbook?"

"I never even took it out of the backpack," said Pete.

"Oh, no!" groaned Bennet, placing his hands over his face. "That means we have stolen property on us! If we get caught with that yearbook, it'll look like *we* stole it! Step on it, Emma!" he cried.

Bennet was absolutely miserable. Everything was going wrong. As he thought about all the trouble they were in, he slumped down into his seat. His foot suddenly touched something under the front seat. A keyboard.

C-mail!

He had forgotten that the Nickowskys' car was equipped with c-mail. Bennet picked up the keyboard. Unbuckling his seat belt, he leaned into the space between the two front seats and plugged the keyboard's cord into the dashboard cigarette lighter. Then he attached the other wires that were underneath the dashboard.

"Quick, write something!" he said, tossing the keyboard into Pete's lap.

"Write *what?*" asked Pete.

"I don't know. Y-y-you're the writer! Write something!"

"What is this thing?" asked Elizabeth.

"It's c-mail," replied Pete. "It lets you write messages in your rear window."

"W-w-will you just write!" cried Bennet.

Pete began typing. He sent his message to print.

Bennet swung around to see what would happen. Nothing did. Mr. Abbott kept right on tailgating them.

"Wh-wh-what did you write?" asked Bennet.

"I told him we're going to sue him," said Pete.

"You jerk!" cried Emma. "Now you've really got him mad!"

"Hey, I was just trying to help," replied Pete.

Elizabeth grabbed the camcorder that was sitting on the seat beside her. She thrust it into Bennet's hands. "Quick, start filming Mr. Abbott," she said.

"What for?" asked Bennet. "The battery's dead, remember?"

"I know that," said Elizabeth. "Look, we bluffed our way into trouble. Maybe we can bluff our way out."

"A bluff on a bluff!" cried Pete. "Hey, I like it!"

Bennet rolled down his window and stuck his head out. He put the camcorder to his eye and pretended that he was filming Mr. Abbott's Jeep.

Emma went ballistic. "What are you doing?" she shrieked. "Get your head back in this car!" But Bennet paid no attention.

Elizabeth, meanwhile, took the keyboard and placed it on her lap. She typed something. "Now what do I do?" she asked.

"Hit RETURN," instructed Pete.

Elizabeth pressed the RETURN button.

Bennet just prayed that Elizabeth's idea would work. He peered through the camcorder's viewfinder. At first, nothing happened. But then Mr. Abbott's Jeep began to slow down. The right blinker on the vehicle started to flash. The Jeep turned down a street and disappeared.

"Hey, h-he-he's turning!" shouted Bennet excitedly as he pulled his head back into the car. "He-he's gone!"

Emma stopped the car. She wiped tears from her eyes.

"What did you write?" Pete asked Elizabeth.

Elizabeth replied, " 'How about a nice big smile for the police?' "

THE CONFESSION

Emma, furious, hit the steering wheel with the palms of her hands. "That jerk was following us way to close!" she said. "I'm finding a phone and calling the police."

She started up the car.

"Wait!" cried Elizabeth. "I have my mom's cell phone on me." She unzipped the outside pocket of her backpack and pulled out a sleek, black, ultra-thin phone. She waved it in the air so Emma could see. "I'll call the police." She was about to press the "9" in 911 when the phone bleated.

Elizabeth peered up, startled. She pressed the SEND button, pushed her hair back, and placed the phone to her ear. "Hello?" she said.

Her eyes widened. She looked scared. She yanked the phone away from her ear and pushed the button that disconnected the signal.

"Wh-wh-who was it?" asked Bennet.

"Mr. Abbott!"

"Abbott!" cried Pete.

"H-h-how'd *he* get your cell-phone number?" asked Bennet.

"I gave it to him."

"You *what?*" cried Emma in disbelief.

"Why on earth did you do that?" asked Pete.

"In case he needed to get hold of us while we were driving over to his house to interview him," said Elizabeth.

Suddenly the phone bleated again.

Elizabeth flung the phone away from her like it was a poisonous snake. It landed on the car seat beside Pete.

It kept on bleating.

"What is this guy's problem?" demanded Emma.

Pete picked up the phone, pressed the SEND button, and cried, "Leave us alone!"

Instead of hanging up, though, he listened.

"Wh-wh-what's he saying?" asked Bennet.

"He's telling me how sorry he is," whispered Pete.

"Oh, I bet he is," said Emma in a very skeptical voice.

"No, I think he means it," said Pete. "He says he didn't mean to lose his cool."

Speaking into the phone, Pete said, "Yeah, we're all okay."

He listened.

"Wh-wh-what's he saying now?" asked Bennet.

"He's asking us not to go to the police," said Pete. "He says his political career will be ruined."

"Yeah, well, he should've thought of that before he started following us," said Emma.

Pete, his ear to the phone, cried, "Hey, he says he'll pay us for the film in our camcorder!"

"But we didn't fil—" Elizabeth started to say, when Bennet cupped his hand over her mouth.

"I have an idea," he whispered. "Here, give me the phone."

Pete handed it to him. "Mr. Abbott, this is Bennet," he said. "Tell you what. We'll destroy the film and we won't go to the police if—"

"What do you mean we won't go to the police?" blurted out Emma. "Hey, speak for yourself!"

Pete waved his hands at Emma to shush up.

"W-we just need to know one thing," continued Bennet, speaking into the phone. "Did you have anything to do with the pumpkin that's up on the Town Hall flagpole?"

"You have to understand," said Mr. Abbott on the other end. "In my wild and crazy youth, I did wild and crazy things."

"What's he saying?" asked Pete.

Bennet placed his hand over the cell phone and whispered, "He's telling me about his college days."

"What's *that* got to do with anything?" asked Emma.

"But that's all behind me now," Mr. Abbott said.

"He says it's all behind him now," reported Bennet.

Pete couldn't resist. "*Behind* him?" he said, grinning.

"Look, Mr. Abbott, we don't care about what you did in college," said Bennet. "We really don't. All we care about is finding out who put the pumpkin on the Town Hall flagpole."

"If people found out what I did in college, I'd be the laughingstock of the town," said Mr. Abbott.

"We're not going to write about that, Mr. Abbott," said Bennet. "We're just interested in the pumpkin."

"When I heard that you had been in touch with my old professor, I just lost my temper," said Mr. Abbott.

Bennet couldn't help feeling sorry for Mr. Abbott. There were times when he, too, had lost his temper and said or done things for which he was sorry about later. Still, they had a mystery to solve. "The pumpkin?" he persisted.

"But I'm a different person now," insisted Mr. Abbott. "I want to fix up the parks and set a good example for today's youth. I really do."

"Okay, Mr. Abbott," said Bennet. "I guess we'll just have to go to the police and—"

"Yes, I put the pumpkin up on top of the flagpole," confessed Mr. Abbott.

"He says he did it!" Bennet whispered excitedly to Pete and Elizabeth. "He put the pumpkin on the flagpole!"

"*Yesss!*" cried Pete. He and Elizabeth gave each other a high five.

"Good job, Alva!" said Elizabeth.

Alva? Bennet thought he was hearing things. Had Elizabeth really called him Alva? He suddenly realized that Mr. Abbott was still talking to him on the phone.

"He says he'll admit it to us if we'll destroy the film and don't go to the police," said Bennet.

"Tell him yes!" said Pete.

Emma tried to say something. This time, Pete *and* Elizabeth shushed her up.

"Mr. Abbott?" said Bennet into the cell phone. "You have a deal." He said good-bye and ended the call.

"We did it!" Bennet said. Smiling, he gave the phone back to Elizabeth.

"Ex*cuse* me," said Emma. "*You* may have agreed not to go to the police, but *I* didn't."

"Y-y-you can't go to the police!" cried Bennet.

"I can so," she replied.

"But if you go to the police, we'll lose our story," said Elizabeth.

"And the prize money," said Pete.

"Prize money? What prize money?" said Emma.

"The prize money we'll get for solving the pumpkin mystery," replied Elizabeth.

"What are you talking about?" Emma asked.

"*The Sun* is of-f-fering a five-hundred-dollar prize to anyone who solves the Town Hall pumpkin mystery," said Bennet. "And we just solved it."

Emma looked confused. "We did?"

"Mr. Abbott just admitted that he put the pumpkin up on the flagpole," said Elizabeth.

"He did?"

"Yes, he did!" said Pete.

"But the only way he'll admit to doing it is if we keep our mouths shut," said Elizabeth.

"You know, Emma, you'll get some of the prize money, too," said Pete. "Won't she, guys?"

"Oh, sure," said Elizabeth.

"Absolutely!" cried Bennet.

"I will?" said Emma.

"Well, of course," said Pete. "You drove us here. You helped us solve the mystery."

"Let's see," said Bennet. "Split four ways . . . that would be one hundred and twenty-five dollars apiece."

"Gee, just think of all the clothes you could buy at Old Navy," said Pete.

"Okay," agreed Emma. "I'll keep my mouth shut."

PAGE-ONE STORY

The next day, Sunday, was cold, rainy, and overcast. But it didn't matter to Bennet, Pete, and Elizabeth, who spent almost the entire day up in Bennet's bedroom, writing their article on Mr. Abbott.

The story appeared the next morning in a special edition of *The Purple Patch* as well as on the Deep Doo-Doo Web site.

Before Bennet left for school, he told his father to be sure to check out the Deep Doo-Doo Web site. "I think you'll find it very interesting," he said.

Mr. Ordway logged on to the Web site that morning at work. He was shocked at what he read.

Just before noon, the principal's secretary came into Bennet's science class and handed the teacher a note. She unfolded it, read it, and then handed it to Bennet. The note asked Bennet to call his father at lunchtime.

"I checked out your story," said Mr. Ordway when Bennet called him from the principal's office. "Abbott admits to it. How on earth did you figure out it was him? And how'd you ever get him to confess?"

"Hey, wh-what can I say?" said Bennet. "We're good!"

"I'll say you are," said Mr. Ordway.

Mr. Vreeland was also very impressed by their reporting skills. In social-studies class, he had Bennet, Elizabeth, and Pete stand up in front of the class.

"This is what teamwork is all about," he said. He had the whole class give them a big hand.

It was pretty embarrassing, actually.

The Abbott story made the front page of *The North Agaming Sun* on Tuesday morning. The story, which Mr. Ordway himself wrote, included an interview with Mr. Abbott. True to his word, Mr. Abbott confessed to the pumpkin mystery. When asked why he climbed the flagpole, he simply replied, "Because it was there."

In his article, Mr. Ordway credited both *The Purple Patch* and the Deep Doo-Doo Web site for breaking the story. This generated many e-mails to the Web site. One of the e-mails came from a man in Springfield, Massachusetts, who asked if the Dracula mask that was on eBay was *the* genuine Deep Doo-Doo Dracula mask. Bennet had no idea what he was talking about. So he went to the eBay Web site. And there it was—his old Dracula mask! The Mad Poet was auctioning it off!

"Authentic Dracula Mask from the Deep Doo-Doo TV Broadcasts," it said above the photograph.

As if that wasn't shocking enough, the Mad Poet was asking $750 for the mask! So *that's* why he wanted it! No wonder the Mad Poet wasn't interested in solving the pumpkin mystery and winning the $500 prize. He thought he could make even more money from Bennet's old Dracula mask.

Another e-mail that came in was from the Mad Poet himself. It was a short poem, a mere two lines.

Although Bennet didn't know it at the time, it would be the last e-mail the Deep Doo-Doo Web site would receive from the Mad Poet.

I think South America would be a nice
place to find a job.

Bennet was tempted to tell the Mad Poet that he really should have told him why he wanted the

Dracula mask. But Bennet didn't. Instead, he just typed:

Thanks.

That same day, Mr. Abbott, to his surprise, received a mysterious package in the mail. It was a plain brown envelope without any return address. There wasn't even a letter or any sort of note inside the envelope. There was just one item—his old college yearbook.

• • •

That night a cold front moved in from the Great Lakes region, bringing an end to the unseasonably mild temperatures. The front brought strong gusty winds and snow flurries. In the morning, Bennet woke up and found the whole neighborhood white with snow. It was the first snow of the season. While it was just a dusting, it was still pretty exciting.

But that wasn't the only discovery that morning.

Over at Town Hall, the custodian arrived at work and found chunks of orange pumpkin splattered on the cement sidewalk in front of the main entrance to the big brick building. Peering up, he saw that the pumpkin was no longer perched atop the flagpole. Apparently, during the night, the gusty wind had blown it off. It was as if the pumpkin had been just waiting for someone to figure out how it got up there. Now that the mystery had been solved, the pumpkin had let go of the flagpole, smashing to smithereens on the ground.

THE CEREMONY

In all the excitement, Bennet and Elizabeth had totally forgotten about their Civil War project. But Mr. Vreeland hadn't. He reminded them that they still needed to hand it in. Bennet and Elizabeth got busy working on it that very afternoon. It didn't take long to finish. After solving the pumpkin mystery, Bennet found that working with Elizabeth on a Civil War project was a piece of cake.

A few days later, *The North Agaming Sun* held a small ceremony in its offices. At the ceremony, Mr. Stevenson, the publisher, presented four checks—one to Bennet, Pete, Elizabeth, and Emma. Each check was in the amount of $125. The parents of the children were all on hand, looking very pleased and very proud. A photographer from *The Sun* snapped photo after photo as Mr. Stevenson, with a big grin, handed out the checks and shook each child's hand.

After the presentation, Elizabeth asked if she

could have a tour of the newspaper facility. Trombly, the editor-in-chief of *The Sun,* was only too happy to oblige. He led the whole group around the newsroom and the other parts of the building. At one point, while they were passing through the pressroom, Pete spotted a stack of newspapers sitting on a long table. He went over and picked one up. It was the next day's paper. It still smelled of fresh ink. The big news was that, in the most recent poll, Mr. Abbott had taken a commanding lead in the mayor's race. Apparently, his announcement that he had placed the pumpkin on top of the flagpole had helped his campaign. It revealed a side of Mr. Abbott that the voters never knew existed— that he actually had a sense of humor and an imagination. If he had the ability to put a pumpkin up on a flagpole, just think what he could do for the town!

Pete started to put the paper down when a small article on the front page caught his eye.

"Hey, listen to this," he said, walking over to Bennet and Elizabeth. He read aloud:

Bike Thief Arrested

A North Agaming man was arrested last night after accidentally tripping off a burglar alarm in a Hill Street residence. John Bilger of 53 Claremont Avenue was taken into police custody as he was attempting to load a stolen bicycle into his van. Police later raided Mr. Bilger's home and found more than a dozen bicycles in his basement, as well as records, books, and other stolen property. In addition, they found a computer and a one-way airline ticket to Brazil. Speculating on Mr. Bilger's motives, Detective William Hardy said, "We believe the perpetrator was selling stolen items over the Internet and that he was planning to soon fly to South America." The alleged burglar is to be arraigned tomorrow on a number of charges, including breaking and entering and robbery.

"The Mad Poet!" exclaimed Elizabeth.

"Sounds like he'll be spending time in jail," said Pete, tossing the newspaper back onto the table.

"I guess he won't be stealing bicycles for a while," said Bennet.

"Or yearbooks," said Elizabeth.

"No," agreed Pete. "But he will have plenty of time to work on his poetry."

Later that evening, to celebrate their solving the pumpkin mystery, Mr. Ordway took Bennet, Elizabeth, and Pete out for pizza. Mrs. Ordway came, too. Emma was also invited, but, being a high-school junior with a car and $125 in prize money, she had other plans.

During dinner, Bennet asked his father a question that had been on his mind for days.

"Hey, Dad," he said. "I have a qu-question for you."

"Yeah, what's that?" asked Mr. Ordway as he took a bite from his slice of pizza.

"D-did you ever streak in college?"

Mr. Ordway stopped chewing and stared at his son. "Streak!" he blurted out.

Mrs. Ordway laughed. "Your father? Streak? Are you kidding me? He wouldn't be caught dead in public without his clothes on."

Everyone laughed but Mr. Ordway. He turned bright red. "Hey, I could've streaked if I wanted to," he said. "I simply didn't want to."

"How about you, Mom?" asked Bennet.

"Not in a million years," she replied. "How do you know about streaking, anyway?"

"*I* know about streaking," said Bennet. "I wasn't born yesterday, you know."

"You kids aren't thinking of streaking, are you?" asked Mr. Ordway.

They all insisted they were not.

"I'm certainly glad to hear that," said Mr. Ordway. "Streaking is one fad I hope never returns. That and disco."

When they had finished eating, Mr. and Mrs. Ordway ordered coffee. Rather than hang out in the booth with them, Bennet, Pete, and Elizabeth went outside to wait in the parking lot. It was a chilly, clear night. A million stars were out.

Now that the pumpkin mystery had been solved, Bennet had thought he would be thrilled not to have to do any more things with Elizabeth. But it was weird. He wasn't thrilled. He glanced over at her, wondering why he wasn't more excited.

She was gazing up at the starry night sky.

"What are you looking at?" he asked.

"Orion," she replied. "See it?"

Bennet peered up at the cluster of stars that Elizabeth was pointing to. It was amazing. For the first time in his life, he spotted the Orion constellation. He had never been able to make out Orion before—or any constellation, for that matter—except the Big Dipper. The rest of the universe was just a lot of individual stars separated by darkness.

"And there's Pegasus," said Elizabeth, pointing to some other stars.

"Check out Leo," said Pete as, head tilted back, he pointed directly above him.

"H-h-hey, there's the dog!" cried Bennet excitedly. "Th-there's Canis Major!"

To Bennet's astonishment, he had connected the stars and found a constellation. It wasn't so hard. In a way, it was sort of like connecting dots to solve a mystery.

Or like connecting one person to another to form a friendship.